A SPECIAL GIFT

MARCIA L. SIMON

HARCOURT BRACE JOVANOVICH

A SPECIAL GIFT

 NEW YORK AND LONDON

Library of Congress Cataloging in Publication Data

Simon, Marcia L
  A special gift.

  SUMMARY: A young boy tries to cope with the diffi-
culties of developing his skills as a dancer and at the
same time maintain his identity as an athlete.
  [1. Ballet dancing—Fiction. 2. Sex role—Fiction]
I. Title.
PZ7.S60519Sp [Fic]   78-4329
ISBN 0-15-277865-9

First edition
B C D E F G H I J K

To Marian Parry—for sharing her art,

and to Sara, Lauren, David, and Jim—for sharing me

The author wishes to acknowledge the gracious assistance of the staff and children of the New Jersey Ballet Company, and to thank Tracy Glazer for her special contribution to this book.

A SPECIAL GIFT

One

"Fly, Peter, fly! Higher!" Peter felt the wind rushing past his ears as he leaped into the air. He came down hard and had to put both hands out to catch himself or he would have crashed into the wall.

"No, no," called Madame Ivanova. "It must be more up—up, and *over*. It is like diving, diving in the air. Keep your chin up and your chest high. Try it again."

Panting and sweating, Peter hurried to the far end of the room. He frowned and bit his bottom lip, then took a deep breath as the music began.

"And-one, and-two, and-go-go-go-go-go-go-go-*go!*" Madame's voice urged Peter into the air. "Let me see you still up there even when you have to come down," she called.

Loud chords of music seemed to fill Peter's head and the air around him. He leaped higher than he had ever leaped before. For an instant he was flying. Then he was down.

I did it . . . I did it . . . I did it, Peter sang to himself as the blood pounded through his veins.

"You did it," said Madame. "You really did it that time. Did you feel the difference? Up and *over?*"

Peter nodded and grinned, wiping the sweat off his face with the back of his arm. He took his place at the end of the line of boys waiting their turns to try the *grand jeté*.

"You were great," whispered John, Peter's best friend in ballet class.

"Yeah?" Peter gasped. "It felt great." Peter leaned against the ballet *barre* and tried to catch his breath.

"No, no, Alec," Madame called to the boy galloping down the length of the room. He skidded to a stop.

"What is this?" asked Madame. "Some kind of ostrich trying to fly?" She imitated his flat-footed run, arms and legs flapping wildly as she jumped. Everyone laughed, including Alec. Peter wondered how Madame could make a kid feel so clumsy and ridiculous without hurting his feelings. She also could make kids do impossible things, like fly, when they had no idea they could.

"We'll do it together, yes?" said Madame. "If you keep your shoulders down, you won't be all over everywhere. You must be just up—up and over."

Madame stood poised next to Alec. She nodded at the pianist in the corner. "And-one, and-two . . ." They were off. Madame took two light running steps, then soared into the air, hung there for a long moment, like a hummingbird, then glided soundlessly back to the floor.

"How can she do that?" Peter whispered to John. He never could get used to Madame's amazing dancing, even though he saw it week after week.

Once, Peter had seen Madame at the supermarket. She was just a short black-haired woman in slacks, pushing a grocery basket. She looked like a regular person, maybe even somebody's mother—definitely not like a creature who could fly. Peter had been too embarrassed to say hello.

"Up, up," called Madame. "Think up!" Alec thudded down

behind her and continued the series of *grands jetés* until he banged into the wall.

One by one the boys ran and jumped, with Madame and the music urging them to pit their strength and skill against gravity. Peter felt as proud at having won a moment of flying in ballet class as he had at scoring the winning basket in gym class a few hours earlier . . .

"Shoot! Shoot! Come on, get it in there!" Peter remembered Mr. Sanford yelling from the sidelines as ball after ball missed the basket.

Peter had crouched and run sideways, keeping in front of Anthony, who was guarding him. He was waiting for the ball to come his way. Then it came—a rebound off the backboard, and Peter had thought it would go over his head. He jumped anyway, springing straight up, and brought the ball down with his fingertips.

Peter remembered the tense feeling in his legs as he pivoted sharply. Anthony hovered over him like an eight-foot-tall octopus. Peter took two quick sliding steps to his right, dribbling low, gauging his distance from the basket. Anthony was on top of him again. With one fluid motion Peter straightened his bent knees, arched his body, and lifted the ball over his head. At the peak of his jump he seemed to stand in the air for a second. Then he released the ball. It grazed Anthony's outstretched fingertips as it arced toward the basket, rolled over the edge of the hoop, and dropped through the net.

Cheering and whistling erupted from Peter's teammates. Hands pounded his back. "'Atta boy, Peter," yelled Mr. Sanford . . .

"Come on, Peter. Turn around." Madame's voice broke in on Peter's daydream. "Don't you remember, for the *tour jeté* you must begin facing backward?"

Peter faced the corner of the room and tried to picture the big jump and midair turn in his mind. Madame clapped out the beat for him:

"And-one, and-two, and-jump-and-turn-and-reach-*glissade,* and-jump-and-turn-and-reach . . ." Madame sang out. "Make your legs cross sharply, like scissors blades."

Peter loved this step the best of all—the quick slide to the side, the sudden change of direction while in the air, the landing on one foot, and the quick takeoff again. It had all the excitement of basketball, but without his having to worry about the ball.

As the boys finished their *tours jetés,* they heard a strange noise—like a herd of cattle crossing a wooden bridge—coming closer and closer. It was the girls clumping up the stairs from the dressing room in their stiff new toe shoes.

The boys slouched against the *barre* and watched the girls as they clustered around the rosin box, taking turns rubbing the toes and heels of their shoes in the yellowish powder. Then they carefully dusted the rosin off the tops of their shiny pink satin shoes, fussed with the ribbons crisscrossed around their ankles and the tufts of white lamb's wool poking out around the edges of the shoes, and turned to admire their feet in the long mirror.

"You should hear my sister carry on about her toe shoes," Peter said to John. " 'Aren't they the most exquisite color?' " he mimicked in a high-pitched voice. " 'Not too pinky and not too peachy? This must be the color of fairy wings.' " John snorted with laughter, then clamped his hand over his mouth. "Some fairy wings." Peter laughed. "She can't move in them. She can't even stand up in them without hanging onto a chair or something for dear life. All she can do in them is look at herself in the mirror, which she does about twenty-six hours a day. I bet she even sleeps in them."

Encouraged by John's smothered laughter, Peter began to imitate the grotesque duck-walk of the girls in their rigid shoes, hobbling and preening in the mirror.

Suddenly Peter froze. Elizabeth, his sister, had caught his eye in the mirror. She shot him a disintegrating look that would have made a Star Trek ray gun look like a water pistol. Peter backed up and joined John at the *barre.*

When the girls were finally ready, Madame sent them to the *barre* for ten minutes of simple *relevés, échappés,* and *passés.* The boys did the same exercises in their soft ballet shoes, but without holding on to anything. Peter could see Elizabeth's knees start to tremble after a few minutes. She was leaning on her arms, her hands gripping the *barre,* as though she weighed two hundred pounds and her feet were worn off at the ankle. Two girls soon collapsed to the floor and sat hugging their feet. Peter saw sweat glistening above Elizabeth's lips, but he knew by the set of her jaw that she wouldn't quit even if blood were spouting out of her shoes.

"Boys," said Madame sharply, "you are so busy with feeling smug that you are not paying attention to your feet. They are flopping like dead fish. Just because you do not have to suffer in shoes that squeeze your poor toes like a vise does not mean you do not have a special job to do. These exercises are to stretch and strengthen your feet so you will be fast and strong. Male dancers must be able to spring high and beat their legs together six or eight times in the air." Madame fluttered her hands back and forth so fast that Peter couldn't count the beats. "When you stand," Madame continued, "all your toes must touch the floor, even the little ones, and when you pick up your feet the toes must always be pointed—like sword points."

Peter was tired. He looked out of the window and saw it was beginning to get dark. If he didn't leave soon, it would be too late to play ball with his father before dinner. After the *reverence,* the elegant bows that always ended ballet class, Peter started for the stairs. He was hardly listening when Madame announced that there would be no class the following week.

"Instead, the auditions for the *Nutcracker* ballet will be held, right here. You must come at the regular time, dressed as usual."

The tired children pressed close to Madame, their faces now wide awake. In the midst of his friends' excitement, Peter suddenly felt that he was all alone. He didn't know exactly why, but he felt uneasy about the *Nutcracker* auditions. He heard the rest of Madame's announcement as though from a great distance.

"This year," Madame continued, "we are very lucky to have Natalie Roberge to be our Sugar Plum Fairy. Have any of you seen her at the ballet?" Several children waved their hands. "She is fantastic, yes?" said Madame. "So I hope you will all come next week and try just as hard as you can. You will be competing against children from the other ballet schools in this area, but I know you will do well. And don't forget, boys, there are as many good parts for you as for the girls. Now go," she said.

Peter led the noisy stampede to the dressing rooms. He sat down on a bench next to John, yanked off his soggy black ballet shoes, and peeled his black tights off his sweaty legs.

"You're going to try out this year, aren't you?" John asked. "You're getting good enough."

"I don't know," said Peter as he bent over to find his sneakers. "I'm pretty busy."

"Oh, come on," said John. "It's really fun to be in a show. You get to dance with professionals and stay out late every night for a couple of weeks. Are you scared of the audition?"

"Of course I'm not scared," said Peter. "I'm just pretty tied up with things at school—basketball and stuff. Ballet is just a once-a-week thing with me." He jammed his foot into a frayed yellow sneaker with inch-deep treads. "I wish this *Nutcracker* thing hadn't even come up."

John gave Peter a quizzical look but said only, "See ya, old buddy." He left Peter alone, tying his sneakers and still feeling strangely uneasy.

Two

"Hi there, sports fans!" roared a big voice. It came from the open window of a green station wagon that had pulled into the ballet school's parking lot. "Peter! Elizabeth! Hop in."

It was Bob Pearson, an old friend of Peter and Elizabeth's parents. He always called them "sports fans," and they always called him "Pearson."

As Peter and Elizabeth climbed into the car, Pearson explained, "Your folks invited me over for dinner and asked me to pick you up on my way."

After he had steered into the steady stream of rush-hour traffic, Pearson glanced at Peter, who was sitting next to him, and playfully socked him in the arm. "How ya doin', sports fan?" he asked in his special way that made Peter wonder if Pearson knew he was supposed to be a grownup.

"Okay, Pearson," said Peter in his deepest voice.

"Glad to hear it," said Pearson. "What about you, Elizabeth?" he asked, beaming at her. "You get prettier every time I see you. Your dad tells me you're terrific at ballet. Can you do all those fancy *pirouettes* and things?'' Pearson raised one arm over his head and cocked his little finger in what he thought was an elegant ballet pose.

Elizabeth blushed, then giggled. Pearson always made her blush and giggle. She nudged her ballet bag, hoping her new toe shoes would slip out so she could show them to Pearson, but they didn't. Pearson had turned his attention back to Peter anyway.

"What do ya say, slugger? Too bad you had to waste all that time waiting for Elizabeth to finish her ballet class. If I'd gotten here earlier, we could have played some ball in the parking lot."

Peter's mouth suddenly went dry and his heart thumped wildly. Pearson didn't know that he danced, too. Why hadn't his father told him?

"Well, I wasn't exactly wasting time," Peter said softly. It seemed as though there were no other sounds in the universe except his own heartbeat and his own voice. "Didn't my dad tell you? I take ballet lessons, too."

"Noooo kidding," said Pearson, raising both his eyebrows.

Peter turned to watch a souped-up red VW Beetle with dual exhaust pipes pass them and overtake the car ahead. He hoped Pearson would watch it, too, and forget about the ballet lessons.

"What do you want to do *that* for?" Pearson asked. He looked as though he had just eaten something that tasted very bad.

"Do what?" said Peter. He tried to make his voice sound casual.

"Take dancing lessons," said Pearson. "What a weird thing for a kid like you to do. I mean, I thought you were a regular boy who . . ." For the first time since Peter had known him, Pearson seemed at a loss for words. Peter kept his eyes on the traffic and hoped no one could hear the pounding in his chest.

"What I mean, sports fan," Pearson said finally, "is that I always thought you were a great ball player and one of the guys."

"I *am* a great ball player," said Peter. "Ballet has nothing to do with that, except maybe it helps my game. I just go to ballet once a week after all," he added. "It isn't any big deal for me anyway."

"I don't see why you have to do it at all," Pearson said. He sounded almost angry.

"It's fun," insisted Elizabeth. "That's why we do it. Because we like the feel of doing it. Anyway, Peter isn't the only boy who takes ballet."

For once, Peter was glad to have Elizabeth butt into his business.

"Well, it's fine for girls," said Pearson. "All that flitting around in short little skirts looks great on girls . . ." Pearson swerved sharply to avoid a stalled car.

"Wow! What a place to park," Peter said. He wondered what exactly "flitting" meant, but he was pretty sure that he had never done any of it.

"What do your teammates think of your little sideline?" Pearson asked.

Peter's face felt hot. Why couldn't Pearson just drop it anyway? "They don't think anything of it," he answered. "They don't know about it."

"Ohhh," said Pearson. "Now I get it. Well, we all have our little secrets—right, sports fans?" He patted Peter on the knee. "I won't breathe a word."

Peter sighed. He wondered what Pearson's little secrets were. He hated to think of ballet as a "little secret." That sounded so dark and ugly. How could something dark and ugly make him feel so strong and free? His muscles still felt good from having danced.

He had tried to think of ballet as something that he just never got around to mentioning to his friends at school. *They wouldn't be interested,* he had told himself. Yet he knew that that wasn't quite the whole truth because he knew that Elizabeth would never tell, either. It was an unspoken agreement they had between them. He knew certain things about her that he would never tell—like who broke the handle off of his mother's crystal pitcher, and who changed a B— to a B+ on her report card before bringing it home to be signed—and she knew never to tell anyone at school about his ballet lessons.

It scared Peter to have to admit now that ballet really was a secret he kept on purpose. It must mean that something pretty terrible would happen if the secret got out.

The rest of the way home, Pearson chatted about basketball. "What position do you play now?" he asked Peter. "You're getting so big these days, I bet you're the center. Right?"

"Actually, I play guard," Peter answered. "I'm pretty fast."

"No kidding," said Pearson. "Did you know that in the good old days when your dad and I were in school together, I played guard, too? And your old man, big bruiser that he was, was one heck of a center. Boy, did we have a team!"

"Last stop," Pearson called a few minutes later as he pulled into the Harrises' driveway. "What do ya say, sports fans? Want to shoot a few baskets before dinner?"

"Sure," Peter and Elizabeth said together. "I'll go in and get the ball," Peter added as he saw his father wave to them.

Peter went in the back door as his father came out the front door to greet Pearson. Peter didn't want to hear the questions he knew Pearson would be asking his father. Why *hadn't* his father told Pearson that he took ballet? He had told him that Elizabeth did. *I always figured that Dad didn't care one way or the other,* Peter thought. *I guess maybe he does.*

As he came back outside with the basketball, Peter heard his father telling Pearson that ballet is especially good for football players. "It keeps you from getting bunched-up muscles, and makes you fast and agile," he explained.

"Oh, yeah?" said Pearson as he pretended to sink a couple of golf balls into imaginary holes. Then he squinted into the setting sun and, with an invisible bat, slugged out a couple of home runs for a stadium full of cheering sports fans.

Peter threw him the basketball, hard.

18

"Pretty good pass—for a ballerina," said Pearson, laughing and shaking his stinging fingers.

"Come on, Pearson," said Peter's father. He was laughing, too, but not looking at Peter. "Both my kids are first stringers. You know that," he scolded, as Elizabeth leaped easily to catch a rebound.

They all shot baskets for a little while, and then went in for dinner.

Three

"Mom, what's L-I-X?" Peter asked.

"Lix?" answered his mother. "I've never heard of it. Is it some new kind of breakfast cereal?"

"No, Mom. L-I-X. It's something in Roman numerals."

"Oh, L-I-X," said his mother, laughing. "Why didn't you say so? Well, as I remember, X used to be ten, and I is one, so IX is—"

"Never mind," Peter interrupted. "I figured it out."

Peter erased his yellow math paper and brushed the eraser crumbs into a neat pile, like an ant hill, in the middle of the kitchen table. A hole had appeared where he had erased once too often. He licked his finger and tried to rub the paper back together with his spit. It didn't work.

"I bet Roman kids didn't have to learn American numerals," Peter grumbled, "so why do we have to bother with Roman numerals? What's a numeral anyway? Why can't they just call it a number?"

Peter's mother was standing at the stove, browning onions and hamburger meat in a large yellow frying pan. The smell made Peter's mouth water.

"Roman numerals are a reminder of our classical heritage. Please get your feet off the chair," she said, all in the same tone of voice.

"What's 'classical' mean?" Peter asked, dropping his feet with a thud. "I thought ballet was classical, but that's all in French. Madame always says the names of the steps in French because she says that French is the language of the 'international world of ballet,' whatever that is. It sounds like some kind of secret club for grownups."

"You're right," Peter's mother replied. "Ballet is classical, too. 'Classical' can mean that something has to do with the cultures of ancient Greece or Rome, like Roman numerals, or it can mean that something has a basic form that is set and unchanging, like ballet."

Peter nodded. "That's one of the things I like about ballet," he said. "It's always the same to begin with. It makes my feet feel good to know that the five positions are always the same, and they can just fall into them automatically."

"I'm glad your feet still like ballet," said his mother with a smile. "I guess that's why I like Roman numerals. They're still the same as when I was your age. New math, old math—it all comes and goes, and no one but a math professor like your father can keep up with it. But Roman numerals are Roman numerals." She dumped a can of tomato sauce into the frying pan and stirred it as it sizzled and steamed.

"But I still hate Roman numerals," said Peter as he turned to his homework, putting his feet back on the chair.

Elizabeth came into the kitchen, a flowered bath towel draped over her head. "Smells good," she said. "I'm starved, and I have to use the phone. Move your big feet off my chair," she said to Peter. "Mother, make him move his feet off my chair. I have an important call to make."

"What do you bet it's to Sharon, the Budding Ballerina," Peter said, taking his feet down again.

Elizabeth dabbed at strands of long, wet hair as she waited for her call to be answered. "Hi," she said. "It's me. . . . Mine isn't dry yet either. . . . I *know* it's less than twenty-four hours until the auditions. That's what I'm worried about. You bring the extra bobby pins and I'll bring the hair spray. I'm so nervous I can't even do a *plié* without my knees shaking. . . . Peter? Oh, he still hasn't decided yet if he wants to try out. 'Rehearsals might interfere with basketball practice,' he says. Can you believe it? Basketball practice!"

Peter looked up from his homework and crossed his eyes at his sister. She ignored him. "He says he's sure he'll get in if he does try out because they're always short of boys. Anyway, he thinks he's good," she said with a laugh.

Peter's pencil point snapped. He went to the pencil sharpener on the windowsill and began sharpening pencils, first the one he had just broken, then several stubs that were in his pocket, then some that were lying nearby. Elizabeth had to shout over the grinding noise.

"My mother doesn't care," she yelled. "She doesn't care about me, either." Peter saw his mother smile to herself. "I'm sure your mother cares enough for both of us. . . . She won't *really* kill you if you don't get in. . . . Well, don't worry. Just think about the beautiful costumes they had last year, and the makeup and the . . . Okay. See you tomorrow. Bye."

Elizabeth turned to her mother. "I'll die if I don't get in," she said. "I'll absolutely die. Especially if I don't and Sharon does. She tries so darn hard. Or you!" she said, glaring at Peter.

"Do you really not care about us, Mom?" Peter asked.

"Of course I care about you, silly," his mother answered. "What Elizabeth means is that I feel you should decide things like this *Nutcracker* audition for yourselves. If you want to do it, and you do pass the audition, then I'll be as proud as can be, and I'll invite my twenty-five best friends to watch you dance."

Peter groaned. "That's the problem," he said. "If I could just be in the *Nutcracker* without anyone knowing, it would be perfect. But if I'm in it, then everyone at school will find out and I'll be finished, for good. The end." He made a slashing motion across his throat with his finger.

"No, that would just be the beginning, dear," said his mother. "You know it takes years and years to become a great dancer. But you're the only one who can decide if it's worth all the work. It's up to you—just like taking ballet lessons in the first place was your idea."

Peter snapped another pencil point. He threw the pencil down. Scooping up his basketball from under the table, he rushed outside, slamming the door behind him.

How can she be so great to talk to about Roman numerals and things that hardly matter to anyone, and so hard to talk to about the things that matter most? Peter wondered. He dribbled up to the garage where the basketball hoop was hung, slamming the ball into the pavement with each bounce. He jumped. The ball lurched toward the basket but missed it by more than a foot. He caught it on the rebound, tried again, and he missed again. He dribbled back to the foul line he had scratched into the driveway and bent his knees. *"Plié,"* he said to himself. Slowly, he raised the ball, using both hands. It hit the ring, rolled all the way around it, then dropped off. Peter sat down on the curb of the driveway.

He pulled up a blade of grass, stretched it between his hands, and blew across it until it screamed. Then he tried to get an ant that had appeared on the pavement to crawl up the blade of grass. The ant detoured around the grass and continued on its straight path. Peter held the grass in its way again, and this time the ant stepped right over the grass and continued on its route.

"You sure know where you're going, don't you, ant?" Peter whispered. "You just have your job to do and you do it. You're lucky you don't have to worry about being in ballets, and what the other ants would think, and things like that. So long, ant."

Peter was startled by the roar of his father's car pulling into the driveway.

"Hi, Peter!" his father called. "Did you have a good day?" Peter shrugged. "Do we have time to shoot a few baskets before dinner?"

Peter's father took off his suit jacket and laid it in the car. Peter tossed the basketball to him, and he caught it easily, with one hand. Peter always suspected that his father had sticky fingertips.

Peter and his father had been playing ball together for as long as Peter could remember, which was since his third birthday. That was the birthday when he got a red fire engine that he could sit in and pedal, and the first of his many baseball mitts and bats. Now they dribbled and passed, guarded each other, and shot baskets with the kind of familiar ease that needed no words.

"What's the matter?" Peter's father asked. "You're not your usual superstar self."

"I don't know," said Peter. "I can't do anything right today."

"Well, what's on your mind?" his father asked. "Did something happen in school? Do you have a big test coming up tomorrow?"

"Well, sort of," Peter said. "The auditions for the *Nutcracker* ballet are tomorrow, and I can't decide if I should try out or not. Rehearsals would probably be on Saturdays, and so is basketball practice once the season gets going. I think I might make the team this year."

"Of course you'll make the team this year," said his father. "You're a natural, a born athlete."

"Well, it's not just basketball," Peter said. "I'm worried about what would happen if the guys at school found out about ballet. So what should I do?"

Peter's father frowned and started bouncing the ball nervously, keeping it close to the ground. "I don't see why you can't just keep up the ballet lessons," he said, "since ballet is certainly good exercise for athletes. But I don't see why you need to do it in public."

"But it would be so much fun, Dad. You don't understand. I love ballet, and being in a real show with professionals would be even more fun than just going to class."

Peter's father stood still, the ball in his hands. "Well, if that's how you feel," he answered, "you should do what you want. You can't go through life worrying about what other people might think about you. Your mother and I have always told you that."

"It's not fair, Dad. It's so easy for Elizabeth to decide to audition. She knows that she wants to get in more than anything."

"Well, I guess ballet *is* more natural for girls, isn't it?" said Peter's father.

"Why does it have to be like that?" Peter asked. "They need boys in ballet, too. It's the same as in all those operas you like so much—they need men, too. Do you think opera singing is more natural for ladies than for men?"

"Well, that's not quite the same," Peter's father answered. Suddenly, he looked annoyed and tired, as though he had had a hard day. "Come on. Let's go in and see what's for dinner," he said.

"Spaghetti," said Peter. "I'll be in in a minute. I'm not very hungry yet." He felt as though a basketball were bouncing in his stomach.

Four

The next day seemed very strange to Peter. At first he wondered if the school clocks were broken. It felt as though it must be lunch time when it was only time for morning recess. And when lunch time finally came, the peanut butter from his sandwich stuck in his throat. He gave up after a few bites and threw the sandwich into a big plastic-lined garbage can. Even his chocolate cupcake seemed dry. He washed it down with big gulps of milk and spent the rest of lunch period outside, shooting baskets with one hand while munching on an apple.

"Hey, are you playing after school?" yelled George. George was Peter's best friend in school, and they played together after classes almost every day when one or the other of them didn't have scouts, religion, a dentist appointment, or some kind of lesson.

Peter shook his head. "Nope. Gotta go somewhere."

"How come you always gotta go somewhere, especially on Thursdays?"

"None of your business," said Peter. "I just do."

Only three kids in the whole school knew that Peter danced.

One was Elizabeth. The second was an older boy in Elizabeth's class who took ballet lessons, too. Peter knew that he would never tell because then Peter would spill the news about him. In school he acted as though he had never seen Peter before in his life. The third person was Sharon, Elizabeth's friend. The main reason Peter didn't worry about her too much was that even though she spent hours at his house playing with Elizabeth and rode in the same car with him to ballet year after year, she never seemed to know that he was a real person. He was just Elizabeth's bratty little brother to her. But he had to admit that she made him a bit nervous. It would be safer if no one knew. Even George might not feel good about being friends with a boy who did ballet dancing.

The afternoon was the opposite of the morning. It passed so fast that Peter could actually see the little hand moving around the face of the clock. Somehow, he found himself in the car with Elizabeth and Sharon without ever actually deciding that he was going to audition for the *Nutcracker*. That kind of thing happened to him sometimes. He just found himself somewhere, or doing something, without being able to remember how it happened. Now, as he watched Elizabeth stuff a banana into her mouth and chew it with her mouth open, a salty taste at the back of his tongue warned him that a bout of car sickness was beginning.

Why don't they have those little paper throw-up bags in cars, like they do on planes? he wondered. He rolled down the window, letting in a blast of cool October air.

"I'm freezing," said Elizabeth. "Shut the window."

"If you'll shut your mouth," said Peter.

"Mother . . ." said Elizabeth.

"Peter," said their mother.

"I mean when you chew," said Peter. "It's disgusting."

"I'm disgusting?" said Elizabeth to Sharon. They giggled. "Girls need energy food, too," she said, and Sharon nodded in agreement. "You know, at school they act as though girls aren't supposed to have any strength," she continued.

"Gym is such a farce," Sharon said.

"Yeah," said Elizabeth. "Everyone just stands around trying not to sweat, waiting for the bell to ring. That's one thing I like about ballet—it matters that we're strong. That's why Madame let us go on *pointe,* right?"

Out of the corner of his eye Peter watched Elizabeth and Sharon arching their feet and flexing their well-developed calf muscles.

I guess I can always back out, even if I do get chosen to be in the ballet, Peter thought, trying to console himself as he stared out the window the rest of the way to the audition.

The ballet studio was packed with children from all the dancing schools in the area. They all wanted to be in the *Nutcracker.* Peter couldn't believe there were so many boys. It suddenly occurred to him that there must be boys in every city, in every state, in every part of the country, in every country in the world, who liked to dance. He had always thought that he and John and the few other boys in his class were the only ones. Now he began counting the boys in the room, multiplying that number times a thousand cities, times fifty states, times a hundred countries. He got all mixed up with the zeros, but he knew it was a very large number of boys. Then, like a punch in the stomach, the other side of the thought hit him: He wasn't so special after all. He wouldn't get in to the *Nutcracker* just because he was a boy and they needed boys. He would have to be one of the best.

Madame announced that there would be a short warm-up at the *barre* before the auditions began. The familiar music and the slow stretch and pull of the *pliés* felt good to Peter, despite his nervousness. The *barre* was so crowded that when he bent forward for the *port de bras,* he bumped his head on the rear end of the boy in front of him.

"Hey, watch it!" the boy hissed.

When the *barre* exercises were finished, Madame introduced the man who was sitting on a stool next to her. He had been watching intently and taking notes in a little black notebook. Peter had wondered who he was. He was tall, with blond curly hair and glasses. His face was broad and tanned, and young-looking when he smiled. He wore a blue work shirt, jeans, and regular brown shoes. He didn't look like a dancer, so Peter was surprised when Madame introduced him as Mr. Corbin, who would conduct the auditions and direct the *Nutcracker* ballet.

Mr. Corbin told the boys to line up first, in two rows facing the mirror. Peter moved into the front row, then wished he hadn't, but it was too late to move back. His heart was beating so loudly that he had trouble hearing.

"This is how we're going to do it," Mr. Corbin was saying. "First we'll do some marching. You're toy soldiers, with your rifles over your left shoulders. Attention! Salute! Forward . . . march!"

Peter felt silly pretending to be a toy soldier, but he imitated Mr. Corbin carefully, keeping his toes pointed as he raised his knees high with each step. Somehow, Mr. Corbin made this simplest of steps look flashy instead of babyish. Peter recognized the music immediately as the "March" from the *Nutcracker Suite*. He had the record at home, and this had always been his favorite section. Mr. Corbin watched as the boys marched, one row at a time. Then he wrote in his little black notebook.

"Okay, that's enough. Thank you," he said. "Now let's learn the beginning of the boys' dance to the 'March.' First I'll tell you the names of the steps, then I'll say them again, with the music. Then we'll mark it out together, just walking through it. Then you'll do it without me, four times in all, the front row moving to the back after each time. Okay. Here we go, starting in fifth:

> *échappé, sous-sous, changement; échappé, sous-sous, changement; jeté, jeté, assemblé, assemblé, royale,* and *tour en l'air.*"

As he said the names of the steps, Mr. Corbin danced them with his hands instead of his feet. After the *tour en l'air* he did a sharp salute. "Got it?" he asked.

Peter nodded. *At least I know all the steps,* he thought. The only really tricky part was the *tour en l'air.* The complete turn while in the air wasn't so hard, but a perfect landing in fifth position was. Peter knew that with these steps it would be elevation and precision that would count. Anyone could just do them. He would have to jump higher, land better, point his toes harder, turn his knees out, round his arms, keep his back straight, hold his chest high . . . He was sweating already.

Mr. Corbin demonstrated the steps again, moving his hands in time to the music as he called out the combination. Then all the boys tried the steps, just marking them out, not leaving the floor for the jumps. They paid special attention to directions, positions of the feet, and placement of the arms and head.

This was it. The separate steps became a dance. They fitted perfectly with the music. Peter wobbled on the *sous-sous* and after the *tour en l'air,* but he finished on the beat with the right foot in front. The second time, his row moved to the back, and he could tell that some of the boys in the new front row didn't remember the whole combination. Now Peter was sure of the steps. When it was his turn in the front again, his heart was pounding—this time not from fear, but from jumping so high. He did it all without much wobbling, knowing he was right with the music. Once more, and it was over.

Now that he was warmed up and sure of the steps, Peter wished he could dance some more. He wondered which steps went with the rest of the "March" music. He wondered who the other boys were. It was fun to jump and turn with such a big group.

Mr. Corbin told the boys to remain in their places while he got their names. Peter's voice sounded loud and high in his own ears as he called out his name. What was Mr. Corbin writing next to his name? Did his smile mean anything, or was he just a happy guy? Without asking himself why, Peter was suddenly very sure that he wanted to be in the *Nutcracker.*

"Thank you very much," said Mr. Corbin. "Those of you who get in will be notified by mail within a week. I hope that those of you who don't make it this year will try again next year. That's all for the boys. Thank you. The nine- to twelve-year-old girls will be next.''

Peter sat alone on the floor near the front door of the studio, reading a Spiderman comic book and munching on raisins from a little red box while he waited for Elizabeth and Sharon. He wished some of the boys would come over and talk to him, but none did. When the girls finally appeared, he rolled up the comic book and shoved it into his book bag along with his sweaty ballet shoes and tights and his slightly soggy homework.

"It was awful, wasn't it?" Elizabeth said as they went outside to wait for their ride home.

"Yeah," Peter mumbled. It just seemed easier to agree than to discuss the whole thing.

"It was so hard," continued Elizabeth, "that I forgot to smile. I didn't even smile once."

"You mean we were supposed to smile?" Sharon asked.

"You're always supposed to smile," Elizabeth replied, "so it looks like you actually enjoy dancing."

"But we never had all those steps," complained Sharon.

"I know," said Elizabeth. "Shar, is this how you do a *temps de cuisse?*" Elizabeth quickly moved her left leg in front of her right, then sprang into the air.

Peter thought she looked ridiculous doing ballet outside in a jacket, her arms loaded with school books. He hoped no one he knew would drive by and see them. Just being outdoors with Elizabeth reminded him of all the problems lying in wait for him if he did get into the *Nutcracker*—and all of them just because he was a boy. Elizabeth didn't appreciate how easy she had it. When she dropped one of her books, he grabbed it and ran toward the far end of the parking lot.

"Brothers are so boring," he heard her say to Sharon.

It wasn't any fun teasing Elizabeth when she was in that kind of mood, so Peter waited by himself for his mother to pick him up.

"Well, how did it go?" she asked cheerfully as soon as he and Elizabeth were in the car.

"Terrible," moaned Elizabeth.

"Okay," answered Peter at the same time.

Their mother laughed.

"But I might just stick to basketball anyway," Peter added quickly. He didn't know why he said that; it just came out. He didn't say another word the rest of the way home.

"Well, I just have to get in," Elizabeth said. "I want it more than anything. And I don't just want to be a clown or a mouse or something, either. I want to be a child in Act I, with a silk dress and lots of dancing."

"I'm sure you did well," said her mother. "You dance beautifully."

Peter wished Elizabeth would be quiet so he could pay attention to his own thoughts, but she continued to worry and complain. "Madame says that success in ballet doesn't always depend on things you can do something about. She says that being born with beautiful feet, or just being the right size for a part, can make all the difference. It isn't fair."

"Well, as long as you tried your hardest," her mother murmured in her most comforting voice.

A lot of good that does, Peter thought. *Trying my hardest might be the worst thing I ever did.*

He tried to imagine exactly what he was afraid would happen if he did get to dance in the *Nutcracker* and everyone did find out. Suddenly, he remembered a boy who had enrolled in his school last year. His name was Malcolm, and he came from some foreign country. Malcolm seemed friendly at first. At least he smiled a lot. But he had one problem—he was fat. No one sat next to him at lunch unless there was no place else to sit, and even though he had a pretty good throwing arm, no one chose him to be on their team unless there was nobody else left to choose and the teacher said, "Guess you get Malcolm. Give it a try, Malc." Even the teachers didn't seem to like him much, which was funny because he always said "Yes, ma'am" or "No, ma'am" instead of "Yeah" or "Nope," and he was very smart, and he never got into trouble. The worst of it was that no one would even fight with Malcolm, so he never had a chance. As he walked home from school alone, kids just called him names, from far enough away so he could pretend he didn't hear. "Oink-oink," they said. "Tubby. Baby face." Peter clenched his jaw as he remembered the terrible words. "Pretty boy . . . fairy . . . faggot." Malcolm moved away at the end of the year. "Poor Malcolm," Peter whispered to himself.

Five

"Do you think you'll get in?" Elizabeth asked Peter as they went into the house together after school.

"Of course we'll get in," Peter answered. "Dad says they'll have plenty of tickets at the door."

"I mean get into the *Nutcracker*," Elizabeth said.

"Oh, who cares about that?" Peter said. "I thought you meant the basketball game that Dad and I are going to tonight."

"Don't you ever think about anything besides basketball?" Elizabeth asked. She stood right next to Peter so he would be sure to notice that she was still at least two inches taller than he was.

"Sure," Peter answered. "Sometimes I think about football. In the spring I start thinking about baseball. I think—"

"Oh, who cares what you think," she said. *"I* think I'm going to go crazy if I don't get a letter today from that Mr. Corbin. It's Tuesday already. On Thursday it'll be a week."

Peter didn't even watch as Elizabeth flipped through the mail that lay on the hall table. She sighed and groaned as her mother came to hug her.

"Hi, Mom," Peter called as he sprinted up the stairs. "Dad and I have to eat early tonight. Game starts at seven."

It was a rare treat for Peter to go out alone with his father at night. It was chilly when they left the house, and the air smelled of dry leaves and damp earth. Everything shone in the light of a huge, golden moon that hovered over the treetops.

"Look how the moon is following us," Peter said, laughing, as they drove down the street.

He turned on the car radio and found his favorite rock station. Peter's father listened to operas at home, but he seemed to enjoy rock music in the car.

"How can you like such different kinds of music?" Peter asked.

"It's called having eclectic taste," his father answered with a smile.

"Oh, the same as my liking ballet and basketball?" Peter asked.

"Um," his father said. "Hey, wait till you see the new forward we have this year. He's our own Dr. J."

The basketball game was at Weston College, where Peter's father taught mathematics. When they arrived, the parking lot was jammed, but they zipped into a parking space right near the gym marked "Reserved for Faculty—Violators will be Towed." Peter checked to be sure that his father's faculty parking sticker was clearly visible on the windshield.

Peter always felt important when he went to the college because almost everyone seemed to know his father. Tonight he was afraid they would never get seats because so many people stopped his father to talk.

"Hi, there, little professor," the ticket-taker said to Peter when he and his father finally got to the door. Even the custodian mumbled something about "Chip off the old block" and winked at Peter. Peter felt sorry for his father. It must be hard to be a mathematical genius and know that your own kid practically needs a calculator to add two and two.

Peter climbed up the metal bleachers right behind his father. They stepped over knees and feet, piles of coats and school books, until they found room to sit together near the top of the stand.

"Think you can see okay from here?" his father asked.

"Sure," said Peter. "I like to be up high." He took his jacket off, rolled it up, and sat on it.

"I think we're going to have a first-rate team this year," his father said. "I stopped in to watch them practice the other day, and they really moved well together. What's the matter?"

Peter was standing up and going through his pockets. "Nothing. I'm just hungry," he said, "and I thought I brought a quarter with me."

"How could you be hungry?" his father laughed. "We finished dinner not more than twenty minutes ago." He handed Peter a dollar bill. "Live it up—and bring me back a chocolate-covered vanilla bar—and some change, please."

" 'Scuse me . . . 'scuse me . . . 'scuse me . . ." Peter said as he bounded nimbly down the bleachers.

By the time he returned to his seat, with a can of Dr Pepper and a box of Cracker Jack for himself and the ice cream for his father, the Weston team was out on the floor, warming up.

"Keep your eye on number 40," Peter's father advised. "He's the forward I was telling you about. Look at the easy way he has with that ball. Look at that jump—like he has springs on his shoes. Look at that follow-through. Find me a dancer more graceful than that. And just think, he's only a freshman. He's 6'4" already, and probably still growing!"

"Wow," Peter said. Then he caught his breath. The opposing team, from Downing College, was loping onto the floor. "What are these guys? Some kind of giants?" he asked.

The Downing players were so tall that, in comparison, their coach looked like a little boy—a sauve little boy with a moustache all buttoned up in a khaki leisure suit. Even the Weston team, which a moment ago had seemed well above average in height, suddenly looked like a team of midgets. Peter had to laugh when the referees ran onto the court. In their black and white striped shirts they looked like little bugs darting between the Downing players.

"I wonder what they feed them at that school," his father said. "But don't worry. We have fine talent, superior strategy, and . . ." He stopped talking and just sat quietly, nibbling the chocolate off of his ice cream, as the Downing team went charging into its warm-up routine.

Using five or six balls at once, Downing passed and shot with startling accuracy. Within seconds, the net under their hoop was bulging, and the balls had to take turns dropping through.

The Weston players seemed to be paying almost as much attention to the Downing team as to their own warm-up plays. They fumbled passes and tripped over each other as their coach yelled directions at them through cupped hands. Their basket seemed too high for them; it remained empty most of the time.

Things didn't change much when the buzzer sounded and the opposing centers jumped for the ball. In thirteen seconds, according to the digital clock on the wall, Downing had its first basket. Downing's defense proved as devastating as its offense. When Weston got the ball, Downing guards loomed everywhere, making it impossible for the Weston players to do anything but hold the ball or dribble in place. Only number 40 played with any confidence; he was able to pump in a few baskets from the free-throw line. The rest of the Weston team seemed helpless as Downing passed the ball above their heads and down the court. The ball shot from player to player as though propelled by taut rubber bands, and with a mere flick of the wrist it was dropped into the hoop.

At half-time the score was 13–40. Cheerleaders fanned out across the floor. "Yeah, Weston! Yeah, Weston! Get in there and fight!" they chanted.

Peter put his head next to his father's. "What are you staring at?" he asked. "That cute one with the long blond hair?"

His father sighed. "The cheerleaders are more coordinated than the team, aren't they?"

"I'm going to tell Mom on you." Peter laughed.

"Do you want to leave?" his father asked him. "We're getting trounced. This is a slaughter."

"So what?" Peter replied. "It's fun anyway. Don't take it so hard, Dad. This isn't *your* old college team."

They stayed until the beginning of the last period. Downing had chalked up a score of 62 to Weston's 23. The crowd was stamping its feet, making the bleachers shudder and rumble like thunder, as Peter and his father picked their way cautiously down to the floor.

In the car on the way home, Peter let his father sing one of his opera arias in his deep, off-key voice. Peter usually turned on the radio as soon as his father cleared his throat, but tonight he just said, "Poor Dad," and opened his window a little to let the sound escape.

They entered the house quietly, thinking that everyone was in bed because there were no lights on downstairs.

"What's that?" Peter's father asked. Someone was playing music.

"It's the *Nutcracker,*" said Peter. "It's probably Elizabeth."

He followed the sound into the living room. Elizabeth was sitting on the couch in the dark, listening to their old *Nutcracker* records. Peter switched on a lamp.

"Hey, turn it off," Elizabeth said, shielding her eyes with her hand. "We don't need it. Look how bright the moon is."

Peter turned the light off and sat down on the floor. He picked up the record album. It had belonged to their mother when she was a little girl. The records were heavy old "78's." Peter rubbed his finger along the gold lettering stamped on the spine of the frayed, cloth-covered album— *"The Nutcracker Suite* by P. I. Tchaikovsky." As his eyes became accustomed to the moonlight, Peter could see the picture on the front of the album. It was of an old-fashioned girl hugging an ugly, wooden doll with a bandage tied around its head. Peter hadn't looked at this picture since he was little. The picture had seemed strange then, even a bit scary. He had wondered why such a pretty little girl, in a fancy dress and long curls, had to play with such an ugly, wounded doll. Now Peter had to laugh at the memory of his childish self. This wasn't a doll. It was the nutcracker itself, made in the shape of a toy soldier. It cracked nut shells between its jaws. In the ballet it gets broken and is tied back together with a handkerchief bandage.

Elizabeth was looking at the program from last year's performance of the *Nutcracker* ballet.

"Can you believe it?" she asked. "This year our names might be right on this list."

"This is my audition music," said Peter, as the "March" began. He kicked off his sneakers and stood up straight, his feet crossed neatly in fifth position, waiting. As the music repeated, he did the whole combination of ballet steps he had learned at the audition:

échappé, sous-sous, changement; échappé, sous-sous, changement; jeté, jeté, assemblé, assemblé, royale, tour en l'air.

"You look pretty good," said Elizabeth. "But that isn't half as hard as the part we had to learn," she added.

Peter was jumping around, marching and swaggering, then doing his combination of steps each time the "March" theme was repeated.

"Come on. You be Godfather Drosselmeyer," said Elizabeth. "I'm Clara."

Peter swirled an imaginary cloak around himself and peered at Elizabeth with one eye shut and the corners of his mouth drawn down. His face looked eerie in the bluish moonlight. He cast a long shadow across the silvery floor and halfway up the wall.

Elizabeth giggled. "Now you give me the nutcracker," she

directed. "Here's the part where we pretend to crack nuts and eat them. You be Fritz and try to get the nutcracker from me."

Peter pushed and chased her again until, suddenly, Elizabeth dropped the imaginary nutcracker. "Look what you've done! You bad boy! You broke it. Poor nutcracker," she crooned.

Tenderly, she picked up the invisible nutcracker and continued to dance. "Now we're getting to my audition part," she said. "It's the waltz the girls do with their dolls, in front of the Christmas tree. This is it . . ." She said the names of the steps as she danced, an imaginary doll cradled in her arms:

Sauté arabesque, failli, glissade, assemblé, échappé, changement, changement, changement, jeté, jeté, temps de cuisse—

"I still can't do that right—" she said to herself.

Jeté, jeté, temps de cuisse.

She ended with a funny little skip, and Peter gave her a push. They chased each other around the living room, laughing and still half listening to the music.

"Now the magic part begins," said Peter. "Maybe this year I'll get to see how they make the Christmas tree grow into a giant tree, and how they make the clouds of smoke when the toy nutcracker comes to life."

"Maybe some year I really will get to be Clara," Elizabeth said dreamily. "Then I would be able to dance in a beautiful, long white nightgown with the Nutcracker Prince. . . . Hey, Peter, what does this remind you of?"

"What do you mean?" asked Peter.

"Don't you remember? When we were little?"

"Oh, yeah," said Peter, smiling. "The fire, in the dark."

"Remember when Dad used to make a huge fire in the fireplace?" said Elizabeth. "Then they'd put a big stack of records on the stereo, and you'd run around and turn out all the lights, even the one in the upstairs hall.''

"If I wasn't too scared," Peter added. "I'd have on my Superman cape.''

"And I wore one of Mom's long nightgowns. Remember those silk scarves we used to wave around? We danced and danced in the firelight. That was before we even knew how you're supposed to dance. We just did it anyway.''

"And then we'd make popcorn," said Peter. The sudden memory made his mouth water. "Go ask Mom if we can make some popcorn now.''

"No, you go ask her," said Elizabeth. "It's late.''

"Forget it," said Peter. "It's just that dancing made me think of popcorn. Do you think they'll sell popcorn at the theater for the real ballet?''

"Don't be dumb," said Elizabeth. "Popcorn isn't elegant enough for the ballet. They have little mints at ballets.''

"So what?" said Peter. "I had Cracker Jack at the game tonight. We lost, in case you're interested.''

Suddenly, the hall light flashed on, and their father growled from the top of the stairs, "Come on up, you two. It's way past your bedtime.''

Elizabeth switched off the stereo, and Peter slipped the records back into their paper envelopes. He glanced out the window as he put the record album back on its shelf. The moon was small now, shining down on the world from a great distance. How could this be the same moon as the enormous golden ball that had followed him all the way to the basketball game? It had been so close then that he could almost have reached up and touched it. It was a real thing—like the basketball game itself. The yelling and cheering, the rasping buzzer, the pounding ball and sweating bodies were all so big and real. Peter knew he was the same boy now, being watched over by the same moon, as he danced in the living room, but everything seemed so different. There was music instead of noise, and his feet made no sound at all on the carpet. He played and pretended when he danced, almost as he had when he was little. He smiled as he remembered the day, a long time ago, when he had jumped off the fourth stair wearing his Superman cape. He had wanted to see how far he could fly. Now he winced as he remembered the pain of his crash landing. His mother had to take him to have his foot X-rayed. It wasn't broken, but it taught him that imagining could be very dangerous. Peter shivered in the moonlight and quickly followed Elizabeth upstairs.

The next day, the letters were there—two long business-size envelopes lying side by side on the hall table. One was addressed to Peter and one to Elizabeth. Peter grabbed his and bounded up the stairs, two at a time. He slammed his bedroom door with a bang that shook the whole house. He sat down at his desk and tipped back on his chair until he nearly fell over. Very slowly, he slit the end of the envelope open with his penknife. He blew into the envelope, as he had seen his father do, then pulled out the letter. His hand was shaking as he unfolded it. It was a printed letter, with blanks filled in on a typewriter. It read:

Dear Peter Harris ;

I am pleased to inform you that you have been selected to dance the part of a child in Act I, scene 1 of the *Nutcracker* ballet.

Your rehearsals will be every Saturday at 10:15 A.M. , starting this Saturday. Final rehearsals will be the week of December 15, from 3:30 to 10:00 P.M., at the Grist Mill Playhouse.

If you are unable to attend a rehearsal due to illness or other circumstances beyond your control, you must notify me before your scheduled rehearsal time. Any unexplained absences will result in your dismissal from the cast.

Performances will be December 20, 21, 22, 23, 24, 26, 27, and 28, the times to be announced.

I am looking forward to having you work with us in bringing the *Nutcracker* ballet to life once again this year.

Sincerely,

John Corbin

John Corbin

Peter read the letter again to be sure he hadn't misread it in his excitement. It was true—he had been chosen. Out of all those boys, the finger of fate pointed at him, Peter. He felt as though he were holding his whole life in his hands as he stared at the letter.

Suddenly, Peter became aware that Elizabeth was screaming and shrieking. He heard pounding footsteps on the stairs.

"I made it! I got in!" Elizabeth yelled. "Open your door!"

"Me, too," said Peter calmly, opening his door part-way. "I'm a child in Act I."

"I am *too*," said Elizabeth, smiling warmly at him. "Are you going to do it? Are you going to do it, or are you just going to play basketball?"

"Of course I'm going to do it," Peter answered. "What do you think I am? Crazy?"

Elizabeth looked as though she might hug him, so Peter quickly shut the door in her face. He leaned against the inside of the door and hugged himself. Suddenly, everything seemed so simple. He loved to dance, and he was chosen. What could matter more than that? In his happiness, he couldn't remember what he had been so worried about.

Six

Peter was right. Being in the ballet caused him no problems—at first. On Friday afternoon, when George asked him if he wanted to get together on Saturday, Peter said, "Sure. Why not?"

"I'll be over after breakfast," said George.

"Make it around lunch time," Peter said. Ballet rehearsal was at 10:15. Peter knew he would be home by noon.

"Lazy bones," said George.

Peter just laughed and shrugged his shoulders. "What do you want to do?" he asked.

"I don't know," said George. "There's nothing to do until basketball starts next month. Why don't we just bike-ride? Maybe ride over to the high school and watch the game. It's at home this week. But I'm broke," he added.

"That's okay," said Peter. "We can sneak in. You know how to do it? You do it during the 'Star-Spangled Banner,' when all the cops are at attention. They're so busy watching the flag that they never even see you! My father told me that's how kids did it when he was my age."

"Everybody knows that," said George. "Okay. See you tomorrow."

"See you tomorrow," said Peter. He wished he could grab George by the arm and yell, "Hey! Listen to this! I'm going to be in a real ballet. People are going to have to pay to see me dance. I'll have a costume, and my name will be in the program, along with a lot of famous professionals. Tomorrow's the first rehearsal and I can hardly wait. I hope it isn't too hard, and I hope I won't be the youngest one there. Isn't it terrific that I made it?" But all Peter said was "Bye."

The next morning, when Peter and Elizabeth arrived at the ballet studio, they didn't have time to be nervous. Mr. Corbin called to them right away. "Peter? Elizabeth? Over here." He checked their names off a list in his notebook, then he introduced them to the ten other children who were seated on the floor around him. Mr. Corbin knew everyone by name already. John, Peter's friend from ballet class, was there, and so was Lisa, a girl Elizabeth had danced next to at the audition. Elizabeth sat down next to Lisa, and Peter stayed close to Elizabeth. He recognized the boys from his audition. They all looked big and old except for one boy, Philip, who was just a little kid. *He must be the one who falls asleep behind the Christmas tree in the first act and has to be carried off stage,* Peter decided. *I'm glad it's him and not me.*

"Where's Sharon?" Peter whispered to Elizabeth. "I thought you said she got in."

"She got in, but she didn't get as good a part as we did. She's a clown in Act II, which is okay, too, but she was jealous of us. I think her mother was mad at her."

"Shhh," Peter said. "He's starting."

"Congratulations," said Mr. Corbin. He perched on his stool and beamed at them. "You should all be very proud of yourselves. Are you?" Everyone laughed and nodded.

"I thought so," said Mr. Corbin. "Well, before you get too conceited, let me remind you that the part of the *Nutcracker* ballet that you're in was considered pretty strange when the ballet was first performed in Russia, in December of 1892. In those days, ballet was very official and important. The Czar himself, who was like a king, came to see the opening performance. We don't have anything quite like that in this country, do we?"

"What about the opening day of the baseball season," said Peter, forgetting his shyness, "when the President throws out the first ball?"

"You're right, Peter," said Mr. Corbin, smiling suddenly. "I hadn't thought of that. Ballet was as important to them as sports are to most Americans. Anyway," he continued, running his hand through his curly blond hair, "since ballet was so official, people expected it to be done in a certain way. Usually, ballets were fairy tales, like the *Sleeping Beauty,* or tragic love stories with a lot of ethereal women flitting around in long white skirts—as in *Swan Lake* or *La Bayadère.*" Mr. Corbin tilted his head and waved his arms limply. Everyone laughed.

I guess that's what "flitting" means, Peter thought, remembering Bob Pearson's remarks about ballet.

"That's why," Mr. Corbin continued, "the children in your scene of the *Nutcracker*—children attending a Christmas party, playing games and acting like themselves—seemed too realistic. It didn't seem enough like a real ballet.

"But, as you'll all see," he continued with mock sternness, "being children at a Christmas party, and *acting* like children in a ballet about a Christmas party, are two different things. It's a whole other ball game. You won't believe how hard you're going to have to work to make it look like you're just fooling around and having fun.

"So, instead of just sitting here getting fat and lazy while I do all the talking, let's get to work."

Mr. Corbin jumped up and stretched. Peter noticed that he wore jeans and a work shirt, as he had at the audition, but today he had on black ballet shoes.

"Putting together a ballet," Mr. Corbin explained, "is sort of like putting together a patchwork quilt. Each patch is made one at a time. Then several patches are joined into sections. But no one can see the overall design—the snowflake or star or whatever it is—until every last section is sewn in place. And the whole quilt is strong and beautiful only if each individual patch is carefully made. Each of you must perform as though you're the star, yet you must work together like"—he looked right at Peter—"like an all-star team.

"Putting together a ballet is the hardest work I know," Mr. Corbin concluded. " 'John, you must be crazy,' I say to myself every night, when my feet hurt and my muscles ache and my head throbs. But then a little voice from deep inside whispers, 'Yeah, but it sure is fun.' So let's get going. Boys here with me. Girls down there with Madame." He pointed to the far end of the long room. Madame was there already, quietly marking out a combination of *glissades* and turns.

The six boys warmed up with some *pliés* and small jumps in place. Then they did the dance they had learned at the audition. They all remembered it as well as Peter, except for little Philip. He was left-handed, and left-footed too. Mr. Corbin had trouble getting him to start with his right foot front each time.

Mr. Corbin taught them the rest of the "March." The steps were not hard, although there were a few very quick *assemblés*. Actually, Peter was a little disappointed that there were none of the flying leaps he was learning in ballet class. He had pictured himself soaring high above the stage now that he was dancing with the professionals. *Échappés* and *sous-sous* looked like kid stuff.

Peter had trouble standing still while Mr. Corbin explained things. His legs felt like powerful springs and his feet seemed to have a life of their own. But Mr. Corbin didn't seem to mind at all. He wasn't like the teachers in school who had to have absolute silence and bodies as still as death before they could tell you which page to turn to. Mr. Corbin just went right ahead, and somehow Peter began to feel his energy change the easy steps into an exciting dance.

When the rehearsal was over, Peter went straight home. He was just washing his lunch down with a last swallow of chocolate milk when George arrived. George never knocked any more; he just let himself in through the back door and sat down opposite Peter at the kitchen table.

"What's up?" he asked.

"Nothing," Peter answered, relieved that his mother had left the kitchen.

"Do you still want to go to the game?" George asked.

"Sure," Peter said. "Don't you?"

"I don't know," said George. "I guess so. But it might rain." George examined all the apples in a wooden bowl on the table. He picked out a medium-size one, huffed on it, and began polishing it on his sleeve.

"Rain! Are you kidding?" Peter laughed. "There isn't a cloud in the sky. It looks like a perfect day—from here, anyway."

"Okay. Let's go," said George. "We'd better take some food."

"Forget it," said Peter. "I have enough money for both of us if we don't pay to get in."

Carefully, George placed his gleaming apple back on the top of the pile in the bowl. Peter noticed his grim expression. "Take it," he said. "You can eat it now."

The two boys rode their bikes down to the Oval, the high school stadium in the middle of town. The sun was warm on their backs, but the air was cool. George stopped to check his tires for leaks a couple of times, but Peter assured him that everything was all right. They got to the Oval just in time to see their home team jog out of the school, cross the street, and disappear behind the stadium fence. A cheer rose from the field, and a trumpet brayed.

"Let's chain our bikes here, to this tree," said Peter. "It's almost time."

Suddenly, the crowd was quiet. The flag bearers and color guards must have just stepped out onto the field, with the band right behind them. Peter could picture the American flag, and the blue and gold school flag, flapping in the breeze as they were carried down the field. The band was playing the school song. The melody sounded thin from outside the Oval, but the bass drum joined the heavy pounding of Peter's heart.

"This is the place," Peter whispered. "See where those two bars are far apart?" George nodded. "That's where we can go through."

"But there might be a cop standing right there," George said. A heavy, olive-green canvas was hung all along the inside of the fence so no one could see in.

"It doesn't matter," Peter whispered. "We'll come out behind the bleachers, and anyway, the cops will all be at attention, remember? That's the beauty of it."

"Ladies and gentlemen," came a solemn voice over the loudspeaker. "Your national anthem."

The "Star-Spangled Banner" had never sounded more beautiful to Peter as he edged himself sideways between the metal bars of the fence. One second he was out, and the next he was in. It was simple.

"Come on," he hissed. George was just standing there.

"What if we get caught?" George asked.

"Come on!" Peter urged. They were up to ". . . and the rockets' red glare," and still George hadn't started through. Peter reached through the fence and grabbed him by the arm. "Come on. You're taking too long. Then we *will* get caught."

Suddenly, George was through, too. They both ducked under the green canvas and immediately stood at attention. Peter sang at the top of his lungs:

> ". . . that star-spangled banner yet wave,
> O'er the land of the free, and the home
> of the brave."

"Nice going," George said.

Peter smiled. He was quite amazed at himself. *I wonder if I'm destined for a life of crime,* he thought. *Lying and sneaking are becoming a regular part of my everyday life.*

A long, nervous drum roll, followed by the crash of cymbals, marked the kickoff. Peter and George missed seeing it as they spotted two seats in the sun near the top of the bleachers. During the long climb up, George kept looking back over his shoulder to see if an arresting officer were following him. Peter kept trying not to look down between the boards to the ground far, far below.

"How much time do you think we'll have to do?" George asked when they were seated.

"Go, team," Peter yelled. Then he whispered, "Is it your first offense?"

George nodded glumly.

"Then you'll probably get off with a suspended sentence," Peter answered. "Will you stop being so nervous? You're spoiling the game."

"How come you're not nervous?" George asked. "Every cop in town must be here."

"Do you really think they're all out looking for us?" Peter asked. He was beginning to feel annoyed, and George looked more upset than ever. "I'm sure they just don't want to miss the game," Peter said. But to himself he said, *You really want to know why I'm not nervous? I'll tell you why I'm not nervous. It's because sneaking into a football game is fun compared to sneaking off to ballet all the time. And doing time in jail would be nothing compared to what will happen to me if I get caught sneaking to ballet. I'll wish I had a nice, safe jail cell to hide in then.*

"We aren't going to get caught," Peter assured George, "so don't be so nervous. What do you want first, a candy apple or hot chocolate? I don't want to blow all my money at once. It's better to spread it out over the whole game."

"Who's nervous?" said George. "How much money do you have?"

The two boys ate and yelled their way through the long game. At the end, when their team had won 42–27, they joined the throng surging down the bleachers and out the main gate. They found their bikes just as they had left them, chained to a tree.

So far, so good, Peter thought as they pedaled home in the late-afternoon chill. *I had a terrific morning and a terrific afternoon, and I didn't get caught either time.*

Peter and George didn't sneak into any more football games that fall, though they did manage to pay their way in to a few. Once basketball season got underway, Peter played with his school team every Saturday afternoon. And each Saturday morning during the rest of October and all of November, he went to ballet rehearsals, without any of his school friends finding out.

Rehearsals were exciting at first, with so many new combinations of steps to learn and directions to remember. But everything was repeated and repeated and repeated until Peter felt that even if his head were chopped off, his feet would dance if they heard the music.

Sometimes even Mr. Corbin seemed fed up. "Look, boys," he'd say. "Don't just stand there. If we wanted someone to just stand there, we'd put a costume on a bag of potatoes. Even if it isn't your turn to dance, look alive!"

"He sounds just like our basketball coach," Peter whispered to John. " 'Are you guys playin', or are ya takin' a nap on the court?' " Peter snarled in a deep voice, which made John laugh.

The boys and girls learned to waltz together by watching Madame and Mr. Corbin. *They* didn't seem to mind holding hands, but Peter found his own palm cold and sweaty as he lined up, hand in hand, with his partner, Lisa. Lisa was a good partner—she was shorter than he was, and she seemed to know what she was doing. But he would have liked her better if her hands sweated, too. He kept wiping his palms on the sides of his thighs, hoping she wouldn't notice. Her hands were warm and dry, and very soft.

"And one-two-three, one-two-three," Mr. Corbin called above

the music. "Bend. Bend! Stay together. What's the matter, Philip?"

"Elizabeth pinched me!" he squeaked.

Peter couldn't help snorting with laughter. Poor Elizabeth had little Philip as her partner. At first she had tried to get Madame to give her another partner, but Madame took her firmly by the arm and said, "No, it is very important for the person dancing with Philip to be a strong dancer because everyone will be watching. The smallest boy always gets a lot of attention by pretending to tag along and get into mischief, then falling asleep under the Christmas tree before the party is over. You must help him." It pleased Elizabeth to think that everyone would be watching her, but as Philip began dancing with his wrong foot right on her toes, she realized she would have to teach him to tell his right from his left.

"But I *always* pinch him," she told Madame. "On the right shoulder. It gets him to start on his right foot."

Good old Lizzie, Peter thought. *I'm glad she's not my partner.*

Then, on the Saturday before Thanksgiving, Mr. Corbin made the announcement that Peter had been looking forward to and dreading at the same time:

"Just one more Saturday morning rehearsal," he said. "Then we move over to the playhouse to begin the big push—all day on Saturdays, then a week of afternoons and late nights, too. Are you ready for it?"

Are you kidding? Peter thought as the other children jumped and twirled with excitement. *Even if it's the most fun in the world, how can I be ready for it if it means being kicked off the basketball team and losing all my friends? Now I know how Columbus must have felt—would he make it to the Orient and return a great hero, or would he sail right off the edge of the world and be eaten by sea monsters?*

Seven

It got colder and colder during the first week of December, but there was no snow. Finally, on the Saturday of the first rehearsal at the playhouse, the snow began to fall. By the time Peter and Elizabeth arrived at the theater, snow was sticking to the slate roof of the playhouse and dusting the tall evergreen trees that hovered over the building.

"I may have trouble picking you up," said their mother. "The snow will probably be deep by the time you're finished rehearsing. Here's money for lunch—eat something besides Cokes and French fries, please. Save a dime so you can call me when you know what time you'll be done." As Peter and Elizabeth got out of the car, their mother called after them, "Zip up, or you'll catch pneumonia!"

Peter and Elizabeth ran through the falling snow to the stage door at the back of the building. As he ran, Peter tried to catch snowflakes on his tongue, but his breath blew the snow away, and he didn't get to taste any. Bursting into the warm, bright shelter of the playhouse, he shivered with excitement.

He and Elizabeth were stopped just inside the door by a man

sitting on a tall stool, with a clipboard on his knees. "Names?" he asked.

Elizabeth told him. He ran his finger up and down the lists of names for a long time, until he found theirs. He checked them off, then filled out two identification cards.

"Keep them with you until the whole show's over with," he said. "You can't get in here without them. We can't have just anybody wandering around in here, you know what I mean? We got a lot of famous people here."

As they tucked their ID cards away, Peter and Elizabeth tried to look as though they always rubbed shoulders with famous people and might even be a bit famous themselves.

"Boys downstairs, girls first door on the left," said the man on the stool. He seemed to be able to tell right away that they belonged in the dressing rooms with the unfamous dancers.

Peter went down a narrow metal staircase lit by a bare hanging bulb. He followed the sound of boys' voices until he found the dressing room door. Though he had been to the playhouse several times—for a class trip, to see several musicals and last year's *Nutcracker*—he had no idea that this vast, dark, backstage area existed.

All the boys in Peter's group, along with a few older ones he didn't know, were crowded into a long, narrow room.

"Hi, Pete!" called John, waving from the far end of the room. "Come on down here."

"Hey, this is neat," said Peter as he plopped onto the chair next to John's. "It looks just like a dressing room in a movie."

Counters ran along the two long walls of the room. Above each counter was a row of mirrors lit by bare bulbs in little wire cages. John had already staked out his space on a counter by neatly lining up his ballet shoes, an apple, and one Batman and two Superman comic books. Peter did the same, emptying his pockets of ballet shoes, comic books, little red boxes of raisins, and his new pocket calculator. He had just settled down, with his feet propped up on the counter, when a crackle of static filled the air. Then Mr. Corbin's voice came loudly into the room over an intercom:

"Attention, everybody. This will be an all-day rehearsal to work out stage business, props, sets, and lighting. We want to try the makeup under lights. Everyone will have a chance to get used to the stage. There will be time for the costume people to get all the costumes tried on. But they are not—I repeat, *not*—to be worn on stage until the full dress rehearsal. Act I, scene 1—on stage in five minutes." His voice crackled off.

The boys quickly changed into their tights and ballet shoes. They trooped out, led by one of the older boys who knew his way through the backstage maze. They filed down a long, narrow hallway, squeezing past racks of costumes and pieces of scenery leaning against the wall. They passed several men in practice clothes and ballet shoes, and each one smiled at the boys and said, "Hi." Peter thought they seemed very casual and friendly for grownups.

The boys found the right door, and quite suddenly, just past a console of light switches and a row of gray curtains, there they were, on stage.

"Hi there, boys," said Mr. Corbin as they squinted into the blazing stage lights. "Now I guess we're all here—except for the soloists, who are coming next Monday. Kids, these folks play the parts of your parents," he said, introducing a group of adult dancers. "Parents, meet your kids." Everyone smiled.

"This will just be a walk-through," he continued, "to figure out where things will be." He began by telling the adults how to enter the stage and mingle around the Christmas tree while the children watched, through a semitransparent curtain with a door painted on it, from the front of the stage.

Peter knew it was important to pay attention to all the stage business, to remember who belonged where and which chalk line on the floor marked which row of dancers. But the lights kept changing color and blinking off and on, and the Christmas tree on the stage kept growing and shrinking, growing and shrinking, until the children felt that it was not the tree but they themselves who were changing size.

"I feel like Alice in Wonderland," Lisa whispered to Peter.

"Me, too," Peter whispered back. Then he felt himself blush. How could a boy feel like Alice in Wonderland? *Lisa must think I'm crazy*, he thought, but she didn't seem to notice. For the first time, Peter realized that Lisa had the bluest eyes he had ever seen, and her dark hair was so shiny that it reflected the red, blue, and yellow of the overhead lights.

Peter could see pulleys and ropes attached to the back of the Christmas tree, and he could hear men yelling, "Pull 'er up," or "Let 'er go," but he still didn't understand how it all worked. In fact, the closer he got to the sets, the more magical they seemed. What at first looked solid dissolved into streaks and daubs of paint as he got closer.

After what seemed like days of just standing around, Mr. Corbin finally said, "Okay. Get your costumes fitted, take a lunch break, and be back on stage for a run-through at two o'clock."

When the boys found their way back to their dressing room, the wardrobe lady, Mrs. DeRobertas, was there waiting for them. She was a short, round, gray-haired woman who wore three tape measures draped around her neck and funny little glasses that had glass only in the bottom half. It was hard not to smile at Mrs. DeRobertas because she looked so cheerful herself, and also because she waddled when she walked. She had measured the boys for their costumes a few weeks earlier, and now she had everything ready, hanging on a rack, with a name tag attached to each hanger.

"Philip," she called, tilting her head back and peering at the tags through her half-glasses, "and Peter. Now try them on carefully, dearies. Don't drag them. And don't, for the love of the Lord, don't sit down in them. When you have them on, just line up over here near me, so I can pin up the pants legs. Richard . . . Steve . . . John. . . ." She continued to hand out the costumes.

"Can you believe real kids used to dress like this?" John asked Peter.

They both had gray pants, white ruffled shirts, and velvet jackets with two rows of gold buttons down the front. Peter shook his head. "Oh, brother," he said. He would never admit it, but he was rather pleased with his jacket. He liked the soft texture of the velvet and the slippery-smooth satin lapels. He was glad his jacket was blue, not too bright but not dull, either.

Philip's mother was in the dressing room. She was supposed to help with the costumes, but she was really there to keep Philip under control, which was no easy task. It took two of the older boys to fish him out from under the counter and lift him onto a chair so his mother could wrestle him into his costume.

"Now hold still, dearie," Mrs. DeRobertas said to him, loading her lips with pins taken from a fat pin cushion she wore tied to her wrist. He jiggled while she pinned up his pants and squirmed as she smoothed out his jacket. She marked with white chalk X's where the buttons would have to be moved over.

"Now this is exactly why we fit you young gentlemen last," Mrs. DeRobertas muttered, shaking her head. "It must be that Thanksgiving dinner. A little turkey here, and a little stuffing there"—she poked Philip in the stomach—"can change you a whole size." Philip was hopping around and giggling, and everyone else was laughing at him.

When it was Peter's turn to be fitted, he couldn't stop laughing. "You know who else is ticklish, dearie?" Mrs. DeRobertas asked him. Peter shook his head sheepishly. "If you'll stop squirming, I'll tell you." Peter stood still, grimacing and rolling his eyes at the ceiling. "Little Natalie Roberge is the most ticklish thing I ever have seen," she muttered, a row of pins bristling between her teeth. "We had to make a brand new tutu for her," she continued as she fussed with the front of Peter's jacket. "You wouldn't believe how those Sugar Plum Fairies sweat. Now hang it up neatly," she told Peter. "Who's next?"

For someone whose idea of hanging up clothes was to toss them in the general direction of a hook, Peter did a nice job of putting his costume on its hanger. Then he pulled his jeans and a red plaid flannel shirt on over his tights and T-shirt, and browsed through John's Batman comic book while he waited for John to get ready to go out for lunch.

The dressing room was warm and stuffy and very noisy. Boys of all sizes were just waiting around. Some were dressed in velvet jackets and ruffled shirts, others in red toy soldier uniforms, still others in gray mouse costumes with long tails pinned to their shoulders so they wouldn't drag on the floor. Someone was playing a transistor radio. The beat of a hard rock band blended with Philip's screams. He seemed to be having a tantrum as his mother tried to stuff him into his snowsuit jacket. A fight erupted in the line of boys still waiting to have their costumes fitted, but everyone was too happy and excited to really care who cut in front of whom.

"Come on, let's go," John yelled above the din.

Peter grabbed his heavy jacket and followed John and a few of the older boys upstairs and outside.

A sudden blast of freezing air almost took Peter's breath away. It was snowing very hard now, and the flakes were mixed with tiny sharp pellets of ice. A rough wind blew them inside Peter's collar, up his sleeves, and into his eyes. The boys ran across the parking lot with their heads down, each depending on the other to find the way.

They burst noisily into the first luncheonette they came to, stamping their feet and shaking the snow off their hair and jackets. Everyone in the place turned to look at them. Peter suddenly felt shy, but also proud to be part of that special little group. He stamped his feet again, more loudly than before.

They all crowded into one booth and ordered cheeseburgers, French fries, a couple of orders of onion rings, and Cokes. Only after the waitress left did Peter relax enough to look around. He was surprised to see that Elizabeth was there, wedged into another booth between Sharon and a girl in clown makeup. Elizabeth waved, and Peter waved back with one finger, as inconspicuously as possible. Peter recognized some of the grown-up dancers who were parents in Act I, scene 1 sitting at the counter. He had just met them that morning, but he already felt that they were his buddies.

"How'd you ever get into ballet, anyway?" a big fellow named Dan ask another of the older boys.

"Sister," said the boy, and he blew the wrapper off of his straw. "My sister started taking tap. Then I saw a guy on TV tap-dancing, and it really looked like fun. So I got my sister to teach me. I started going to class with her—there were a couple of other boys there, too. Then my sister switched to ballet and pretty soon I did too. I dunno why, I just like it better. You can move more, I guess."

Peter nodded. "Yeah, I got into it from my sister, too." Everyone turned to look at him. They seemed to expect him to say more, but he couldn't think of anything interesting enough, so he took a drink of water and chewed his ice.

The cheeseburgers finally came. They were thick, warm, and juicy. The boys passed the catsup around and shared the onion rings.

"We'd better watch out that Henry here doesn't try to poison us," said one of the boys. "It isn't much fun being understudy, is it, Hank, if no one gets sick? Remember all that chicken pox last year?"

"What an epidemic," said Henry. "I got to dance in every performance. But don't worry about me—something always comes up." Peter felt strangely uneasy, but he joined in the laughter.

"You know that little kid, Philip?" said the boy who had tap-danced. "You should see that kid skate! I saw him at the rink the other day, and he's a terrific figure skater. You ought to talk to him. He told me all about doing figures and edges, and what kind of music he likes, and what competitions he's won. He takes ballet to help his skating. He's so little he needs his mother in the dressing room, but boy, can he skate!"

"Hey, did you see that guy in the wings while we were on stage this morning?" asked John. "That great big guy—looked like a wrestler or something? He was spinning and spinning like a top. I thought he'd never be able to stop. Then he stopped—perfect fourth position, just like that! I've never seen anything like it. Then the guy shook his head, like he was mad at himself, and he started up again. Fantastic!" John shook his head and sighed.

"Don't you ever go to see real ballet in the city?" Henry asked.

"Uh-uh," said John. "My dad won't take us. 'There is no way,' he says, 'that you're going to get me to watch a bunch of queers in long colored underwear jump around on a stage.' " Everyone laughed loudly, though no one looked very happy. "He probably won't even come to see the *Nutcracker*," John added, and he busied himself with his French fries.

"Well, you're not alone," said Dan. "I read that Villella had trouble with his parents, too. They made him quit dancing for four years, so he became a boxing champ. But nothing could keep him away from ballet—he loved it so much. I read that now he earns $100,000 a year just by dancing."

"What do you think Nureyev makes?" another boy asked.

"I don't know," answered Dan. "Plenty. I read that Baryshnikov will be making $300,000 a year. But he sure deserves it. How many people can fly?"

"Yeah," the other boy agreed. "But most dancers barely make enough to live on. And all it takes is one big injury and it's all over." He sighed and drained his Coke glass.

They talked about ballet until it was time to leave for the afternoon rehearsal. Some of the names meant nothing to Peter— Balanchine, *cabrioles*, *entrechat huit*, *Petrouchka*—but he was very happy to be sitting there, part of the special group, sharing the excitement.

By the end of the afternoon, the playhouse was beginning to feel like home to Peter. When their father came to pick him and

Elizabeth up, he felt as though he'd been away from his house and parents for days.

"Dad!" Elizabeth gasped as soon as they got into the car. "Dad, you won't believe how gorgeous my costume is. It's prettier than I could have dreamed of."

"I'll bet it's green," teased her father, knowing that that was Elizabeth's least favorite color.

"Well, as a matter of fact, it *is* green!" said Elizabeth. "No, it's really white, with thin green stripes. But it's long and silky, with a satin sash and tiny little bows, and lace all over the top. White lace pantaloons and petticoats go underneath. It makes me feel absolutely beautiful."

"Absolutely beautiful," Peter echoed in a high voice. Elizabeth ignored him. "But poor Sharon—all she has is a clown outfit, and she has to wear clown makeup all over her face. She got to try it today, and she says it itches. I didn't get to try my makeup yet, but—"

"Peter," interrupted his father, "do you have to wear makeup, too?"

"I guess so," Peter answered. "Yeah, I'm sure I do. Everyone wears makeup, so the audience can see what you look like in the bright lights."

"You mean you'll be wearing lipstick?" his father asked.

"Yeah, I guess so," Peter answered. "Not just me. All the guys." *Oh what's the use*, he thought. *Just when I'm feeling good, and dancing seems like a normal thing for a bunch of guys to do, this has to start again.*

But his father wasn't finished yet. "Guess who I ran into at the hardware store this afternoon?" he asked.

"I give up," Peter answered sullenly.

"Your coach. What's his name?"

"Mr. Sanford?"

"Right. He asked me why you weren't at basketball today. Well, I didn't know what to say, so I mumbled something about your having a cold, which isn't exactly a lie since you do have a sniffle, and I said that you'd be there for sure next Saturday.''

"What did you do that for?" Peter demanded. "I'm going to be at ballet. It's just for one more Saturday, then comes vacation. I'll only miss one more basketball game.''

"It's just for an hour, Peter," his father said firmly, "and I told him you'd be there. Are you so important that they can't spare you from the ballet for one hour?''

"Oh, okay," said Peter. "I guess I can manage both. Mr. Corbin announced they were going to rehearse Act II first anyway.''

Eight

The next Saturday, right in the middle of the basketball game, something seemed to be wrong with Peter's legs. They had behaved normally at ballet rehearsal during the morning, but now they were going out of control. Instead of running, Peter felt as though he were galloping in an uneven rhythm. He had just stolen the ball at mid-court and was headed toward the basket for a layup when his legs started getting tangled up. Desperately, he searched for someone to pass to.

"Come on, Pete," the coach yelled. "What's the matter? Take it all the way!"

Peter threw the ball to George as he stumbled and went down on his knees, but it was the other team's center who caught it. George bumped into the center, and the whistle blew.

"What'd you do that for?" scolded the coach. "Now you guys have lost the ball. You had it right there, Pete. You could have scored. What's the matter with you today, anyway?"

Peter shook his head and rubbed his reddened knees. His team was losing, 12–15. They really could have used that basket. Now, as he lined up to watch the opposing center, who was almost as tall as a grownup, take the foul shot, Peter glanced at the clock. He'd already been away from the playhouse for almost an hour, and it wasn't even half-time yet.

Suddenly, the ball was coming right at him, a rebound off the backboard. He jumped with more strength than he knew he had, straight up, and grabbed the ball.

"Atta boy!" he heard the coach yell. "Now you're cookin'."

But he came down on the side of his foot, and his ankle twisted under him. He fell, the ball still in his hands.

"Call time out, time out," growled the coach. The referee blasted his whistle.

"I'm okay," Peter said, getting up and bouncing the ball to the referee. His ankle hurt, but he could walk on it. He limped a little more than was necessary as he was motioned out of the game. Maybe the coach would feel sorry for him instead of angry. George slapped Peter on the back as he headed for the sidelines.

The coach started right in on him. "What's the matter with you lately? First you miss a game, then you act like you're spastic or something. I didn't think I was going out on a limb to put you on the team so soon. You have the makings of a first-rate player, but I don't know. Sometimes I wonder."

"I'm sorry," Peter said. "I don't know what happened. I'm really sorry, though." To himself he said, *Don't you dare cry, you big baby!*

The coach softened right away. "Well, don't take it so hard," he said, putting his heavy arm around Peter's shoulders. "Everybody has his off days. Just take it easy for a couple of minutes."

Peter sat on the bench, rubbing his ankle in case the coach was still watching, and thinking that he just wanted the game to hurry up and be over so he could get back to the ballet rehearsal. He didn't even care who won. He just wanted to get away. At half-time, his father came over to ask him if he was all right. Peter told him that he had to leave right away.

"You tell the coach," Peter begged. "Tell him I can't play any more today because of my ankle. You tell him. He likes you."

Peter's father walked over to the coach, and in a minute they were smiling and talking together like old friends.

"No problem," Peter's father reported back to him. "He says to take good care of that ankle. Let's go."

Peter didn't talk all the way back to the playhouse. He was angry with his father for making him go to the game, and angry with the coach for scolding him. Most of all, he was angry with himself—for agreeing to play in the game in the first place when he should have been at the ballet rehearsal, for playing like a clumsy idiot, and for leaving the game to go to ballet when any kid in his right mind would have wanted to stay at the game and help his team win.

He changed from his basketball shorts back into his ballet tights in the car. "I wonder how Superman does it so fast, jammed into a phone booth," he grumbled to himself.

He got back to the dressing room just as the boys from Act I, scene 1 were filing upstairs to go on stage. There wasn't even time for a quick warm-up. He just threw his jacket and sneakers into the dressing room and put his ballet shoes on as he ran to catch up with his group. With enormous relief, he realized he had made it back without being missed. To celebrate, he did a few *pirouettes* while Mr. Corbin found the right section of music on the tape recorder. Peter was still out of breath from his dash to the stage, and in a minute he had made himself dizzy besides.

They began right off with the boys' "March." Peter relaxed; he knew it in his sleep: *échappé, sous-sous* . . . But as soon as his feet left the floor for the *tour en l'air,* he knew that something was wrong. He was off balance, and as he turned around in the air he didn't snap his head around quickly enough. His eyes lost their "spot," and he couldn't tell which direction was front. He landed before completing the turn and stumbled. Then one leg slid out from under him, and he thudded to the floor.

I've just twisted my ankle again, he thought. But when he tried to stand, a hot pain shot up his leg, and tears sprang into his eyes.

He collapsed to the floor, hugging his leg, rocking back and forth, and biting his lower lip to keep from crying.

Mr. Corbin and Elizabeth ran to him.

"That's what you get for fooling around right before you dance," said Elizabeth. Then she saw the tears. She knelt down and put her arms around his shoulders. "It must hurt pretty bad," she said to Mr. Corbin. "Peter never cries."

"Let's see, Peter," said Mr. Corbin. "Can you wiggle your toes?"

"Yeah," said Peter. "It's my ankle. It hurts. I can't even stand up."

"It's beginning to swell, isn't it?" said Mr. Corbin. "Elizabeth, better go call home," he directed. "Peter, my friend, we're going to send you to Dr. Shultz, our company doctor. He takes care of all our professional dancers. There isn't any dance injury under the sun that he hasn't seen at least once. He'll know what to do with you. Don't you worry."

Very gently, Mr. Corbin helped Peter slide himself to one side of the stage. "He'll be all right," Mr. Corbin announced, turning his attention back to the rehearsal. "Let's run through the "March" again. We'll need the understudy. Somebody—Lisa—go find Henry Rieff."

Mr. Corbin ran the tape backward through the tape recorder until he found the beginning of the "March." Peter sat alone on the floor. The sharp pain in his ankle was changing into a throbbing ache. As he watched the rehearsal continue without him, he said to himself, *Guess I should have stayed at basketball after all. They can get along just fine without me here.*

Peter's father received Elizabeth's phone call, as soon as he got home. He had to turn right around and drive through the snow again to the playhouse. He looked so concerned when he found Peter sitting alone at the edge of the stage that Peter said, "Don't worry, Dad. It's only my ankle again."

Mr. Corbin came over, shook hands with Peter's father, and told him how to find Dr. Shultz's office.

"Take good care of that boy of ours, Mr. Harris," Mr. Corbin said. "We need him back soon." He smiled reassuringly at Peter as his father supported him firmly under the arms and helped him stand up.

But Peter could tell that his father was angry by the way he started the car. He revved the engine loudly, then backed up too fast. When he accelerated, the car skidded and the back tires spun against the ice with a sickening scream. Peter slumped in the corner of the back seat, his injured leg stretched out straight, waiting for whatever was coming.

"I told you the coach said to take it easy with that ankle," his father said. "Why don't you ever listen?"

"But, Dad, I had to dance. It was my turn."

"You don't *have* to dance at all," his father said, leaning forward to wipe the windshield clear with his arm. "You ought to . . ." The difficult driving occupied all his attention, and he never finished his sentence.

Peter's window had fogged up, too, but Peter didn't even bother to rub a place clear so he could see where they were going. The pain in his ankle seemed to be taking over his whole body now, and he felt utterly alone.

Though the snow had stopped falling, the sky was still overcast, and the streets were strangely silent as Peter's father drove cautiously through an unfamiliar neighborhood, looking for Dr. Shultz's office. He parked in front of an old, red brick apartment building.

"All out," he said in his usual joking voice as he helped Peter out of the car, but he walked through the snow so quickly that Peter had trouble keeping up with him. Just inside the door, Peter nearly slipped in a puddle on the floor. While his father searched for Dr. Shultz's name among the rows of nameplates on the wall, Peter studied the pattern of the black and white tiles on the vestibule floor. It reminded him of the bathroom floor at school. He never had been able to decide if it was a white floor with a black design, or the other way around. Staring at it made him dizzy. He jumped at the loud, harsh "bzzzzz" that permitted his father to push open the lobby door.

Dr. Shultz's waiting room was all brown—brown rug, brown wood furniture, brownish wallpaper with a bumpy design printed on it. Even the music, coming from a portable radio that sat on top of the radiator cover, seemed old and brown. There were no windows.

No one was in the room but Peter and his father. Peter wished he were with his mother instead and that they had gone to Dr. Lief, the pediatrician, instead of this Dr. Shultz. Peter had known Dr. Lief all his life, and even though he gave shots, he was nice, and his office was cheerful and modern. Here, instead of Dr. Lief's cute little nursery rhyme books and Playskool puzzles, Dr. Shultz had only a pile of dog-eared *National Geographics* and two NO SMOKING signs. There was also a floor-model ash tray with sand in the top—full of cigarette butts. And instead of Dr. Lief's little pink and blue pamphlets on "How to Feed and Care for Baby," there was a rack of the most gruesome pamphlets Peter had ever seen. "PAIN," they said, in blood-red letters. Each pamphlet had a skeleton on its front page. Some of the skeletons were half covered with muscles. Some had red blood vessels or yellow nerves creeping all over them like snakes. Peter wished his father would talk to him, but he seemed engrossed in a red pamphlet called "Structural Spinal Disorders."

"I'm not that far gone yet," Peter finally said. "Let's get out of here, okay, Dad?"

Just then a door opened, and a little old man lurched into the waiting room. He was as bent and wrinkled and gnarled as an old fruit tree. When he caught Peter staring at him, he winked.

"That Dr. Shultz is some magician, some magician," he cackled. "When I started coming here I was a prisoner in my own body. Couldn't move a muscle. And look at me now, sonny. Spry as can be. Dancing away, dancing away," he repeated as he struggled into a long, black overcoat. He winked at Peter again, then lurched out the door.

"You must be Peter Harris," boomed a big voice.

Peter turned in surprise. He hadn't heard anyone enter the room.

"I've been expecting you. I'm Dr. Shultz."

Peter saw a big man, gray-haired, with pink cheeks, bright blue eyes, and a bristly moustache. He gave Peter's hand a long, firm shake in his enormous, warm paw.

"Is this your papa?" he asked, shaking hands with Peter's father. "John Corbin called and told me you were on your way over."

Peter couldn't help smiling at Dr. Shultz. He'd never before seen a man who looked so much like an elf—an overgrown one, but an elf nevertheless. Dr. Shultz was wearing a tunic, the sort of short-sleeved, zippered jacket that dentists wear. But his was brown. Suddenly, brown looked like a nice color. *It must be Dr. Shultz's favorite color,* Peter decided as he looked around the brown waiting room again.

"So, you're one of Johnny Corbin's dancers," Dr. Shultz said as he helped Peter hop into the examining room. He gently removed Peter's ballet shoe and eased him out of his tights. At the same time he asked him how he had hurt his ankle and what it felt like.

At Dr. Lief's office, Peter's mother usually did the talking. If Dr. Lief asked how Peter was feeling, his mother would rush right in with the vital statistics: temperature, number of sneezes, an imitation of his cough. She knew more about Peter's body than he did himself. But now, Peter's father sat across the room in a chair next to Dr. Shultz's desk, and Dr. Shultz was waiting for Peter to answer for himself.

"I just twisted my ankle," he said. "I can't stand on it. It hurts."

"How'd you do that?" Dr. Shultz asked calmly, as though he had all the time in the world.

"Dancing," Peter answered. "We were rehearsing for a show and—"

"No, Peter," his father interrupted. "You did it at basketball. Remember? Peter was playing a fast game," he said to Dr. Shultz. "He had just caught a high rebound when he stumbled. It looked as though he had just twisted his ankle. It didn't seem serious, but the coach took him out of the game and told him to take it easy for a while."

Dr. Shultz continued to examine Peter's ankle. He compared it with the one that wasn't swollen.

"Whichever it was, I think ballet's as dangerous a game as any yet invented," Dr. Shultz said, "judging by the injuries I see. This is some muscular pair of legs you have here, Peter. You must be quite an athlete. What else do you play, besides ballet and basketball?"

His ankle hurt so much that Peter had to dig his fingernails into the edge of the examining table to keep from crying each time Dr. Shultz touched it. He couldn't concentrate enough on anything else to even remember what other sports he played.

Dr. Shultz seemed to read his mind. "I expect that hurts quite a bit," he said, "enough to make a lot of fellows cry. But the pain won't last forever, I can promise you that. I don't think anything's broken, but we'll X-ray it just to be sure."

As he led Peter out of the room, Dr. Shultz turned to Peter's father and said quietly, "This is quite a brave young man you have here, Mr. Harris. I'll have him back to you in a minute."

He took Peter down the hall to a small X-ray room. There he placed a heavy lead apron over Peter's body and positioned his ankle on the X-ray plate.

"Hold still," Dr. Shultz called from outside the doorway. Peter knew that you couldn't feel X-rays, but all alone in the room, the huge black machine hovering over him, he thought maybe he did feel an X-ray or two.

A moment later, he was back in the examining room with his father, and Dr. Shultz was showing both of them the framed photographs that covered the wall behind his desk. There were shots of football players crouching over the ball or kicking high, their legs almost doing a split. There were basketball players leaping toward the hoop, the ball floating above their outstretched fingers. There were hockey players, a baseball pitcher, women and men golfers, tennis players—all bending, stretching, reaching, straining. Their motion was frozen by the camera into poses so much like those of dancers that it was a minute before Peter noticed that there were pictures of dancers there, too.

"You look at my rogues' gallery while I get the X-rays developed," said Dr. Shultz. "My favorite patients are you dancers and athletes. You can see why. You fellows demand an awful lot from your bodies. There's someone you know in those pictures, Peter. See if you can spot him."

Peter tried to decipher the scribbled autographs. Many of the photos were inscribed "To Dr. Shultz." His eyes kept returning to a picture of a male dancer soaring high above the floor, his legs spread wide apart in a *grand jeté*. He had on makeup and a prince-type costume, but his smile and curly blond hair seemed very familiar.

"Dad, can you read this?" Peter pointed to a scrawl across the lower right corner of the picture.

"Looks like 'Gratefully yours, John'," said Peter's father.

"It's him!" said Peter. "Mr. Corbin. I can't believe he can jump like that. I wonder when that was taken. Guess he didn't wear glasses then."

"You mean that's the same fellow I just met at the playhouse?" Peter's father asked. "He looks better without the makeup if you ask me."

"So you found him," said Dr. Shultz as he strode into the room. "Johnny was one of my first dancers. He wrenched his back, then he really did a job on his knee. He'll never again be as good as new, but you will, young man. The X-rays show no fracture, just as I thought. It's only a slight dislocation, which I can fix in no time. Come lie down over here, Peter."

Dr. Shultz was standing next to the strangest table Peter had ever seen. The top was made of soft, green vinyl, supported by a metal pedestal. But it was in sections, as though Dr. Shultz had sawed through a patient lying on it and had sawed right through the table, too. Dr. Shultz must have pushed a hidden button, because suddenly there was an eerie whirring sound, and the sections of the table began to move together. Then the whole table began to tip upward until it stood on end on the floor. Peter didn't have the slightest idea where he was to lie down.

With a twinkle in his eye, Dr. Shultz helped Peter stand on a little ledge attached to the foot of the table, his back resting against the green padding. Then the whirring sound began again, and Peter found himself floating up and back. He held on to the green padding, his eyes wide with surprise. In a moment he was lying down, without having moved a muscle.

Then Dr. Shultz gently took Peter's foot in both hands and gave it a firm pull. It made the ankle hurt even more, but before Peter could yell, it felt better. And that was it. The table lowered itself like an obedient magic carpet, and Dr. Shultz handed Peter a pair of crutches.

"Keep off that foot completely for five days—till Thursday," Dr. Shultz said. "Just wear a warm sock, no shoe. Use plenty of hot compresses—washcloths wrung out in water as warm as you can comfortably stand.

"Let me know how he's doing," he said to Peter's father. "If it still bothers him, I'll see him again on Wednesday.

"If not," he said to Peter, "we'll exercise it a little more each day for a week, and on Christmas day you can dance again and play basketball and swing from the chandeliers. Easy now," he said as Peter swung forward on the crutches. "I'm saving a spot on my wall among the superstars for a photo of you."

Peter was so busy experimenting with the crutches, seeing how far he could go on one swing, that he was out in the waiting room before he realized what Dr. Shultz had said. "Did he say no dancing till Christmas?" he asked his father.

"That's what he said," Peter's father answered. "No basketball, either. Too bad. How many games will you miss?"

"But, Dad, the *Nutcracker* opens December 20! That's a week from today!" The fear that had been hovering over him since he hurt himself now came crashing into reality. "You mean I'll have to miss it?"

" 'Fraid so, Peter. I'm sorry," said his father, but he didn't sound sorry. He turned to get their jackets off the coat rack. "You weren't sure you wanted to dance in public anyway, remember? Now it's decided for you, so you don't have to worry. Of course, if you get better in time for the performances after Christmas, that's fine, if you still want to dance. If not, well, that's okay, too. We'll have a good time—"

"You're kidding!" Peter said. He couldn't believe it. He'd been through so much already just to be in the ballet—deciding to audition in the first place, worrying about what the kids at school would think if they found out, rehearsing instead of playing basketball, all the sweat and hard work. And now, after all that, he'd have to miss the opening performance. "You're kidding," he said again, and his voice trembled.

His father looked at him and saw his eyebrows wrinkle up and his face turn red. "You're not going to cry about it, are you? Isn't it enough that you do ballet dancing without having to act like a baby on top of it?" Then his voice softened. "No sense getting yourself all worked up, Peter. Come on, put your jacket on. I'll help you out to the car."

"I can manage by myself," Peter said, swinging himself slowly out the door on his crutches.

As soon as he started the car, Mr. Harris said, "Peter, listen to me. I understand how disappointed you are at missing your opening. But what I meant was maybe it's just as well—"

"But, Dad—" Peter tried to interrupt.

"Wait a minute. Listen to me. There's something I've been wanting to tell you, to discuss with you, man to man. You know, I've always stood behind you one hundred percent in everything you've wanted to do, right?"

Peter didn't answer.

"When you decided you wanted to learn to ride a two-wheeler, I was the one who ran up and down the street with you a hundred times, even though it happened to be the single hottest day of the summer. Remember?"

Peter tried to laugh, but only a funny, choked sound came out.

"When you wanted more rocks for your rock collection," his father continued, "I was the one who spent his whole summer vacation picking up every weird rock on the beach. Right? When you wanted to make the basketball team, I dribbled and passed and shot baskets with you every day after work, no matter how tired I was. And when you wanted to take ballet lessons, I didn't try to stop you, did I? Ballet dancing is not my cup of tea, but still I pay for your lessons and I'm glad you enjoy them. But Peter—I'm telling you this for your own good—it's better not to do it in public. You're just asking for trouble. You know what I mean."

"But, Dad," Peter said, "it's more fun to be in a show than just to dance in class all the time. It's like playing basketball in a game is more exciting than just practicing in the driveway. It's more fun, and I'm going to do it," he finished in a firm voice.

"Peter," his father answered, "as I said, I'm telling you this for your own good, so don't misunderstand. If you want to move fast and feel strong, if you want to jump and turn in the air, and you want to do it in public—fine. Just take my advice and do it in shorts instead of those tights, and do it with a ball in your hands."

"Well, now I can't play basketball or dance," said Peter, his voice rising. "And it's all your fault! If you hadn't made me go to basketball today, I never would have hurt my ankle in the first place. It's all your fault," Peter yelled, "and you're glad it happened!"

"Nonsense!" his father said. Peter saw the muscles of his jaw bulge and twitch.

"And I think you're more worried about what your friends will think when they find out I'm in the ballet than about what my friends will think. You're afraid people like Pearson will think you're the father of a kid who turned out to be a—"

"That's enough out of you!" his father yelled. "When are you ever going to face facts and grow up?"

Peter held his breath, but he couldn't hold in his tears. He turned his face to the window and cried without making a sound.

Nine

"Crutches!" said George, when he met Peter in school on Monday morning. "How neat. Can I try them?"

"Sure," said Peter, sitting down at his desk. But just then the bell rang. Peter needed his crutches to stand for the flag salute, so George had to wait to try them.

"I thought you just *twisted* your ankle," George whispered. "What did you do, break it or something?"

"I did twist it," Peter said, his voice muffled as he rummaged around inside his desk looking for his math book. "At basketball," he added, pulling out his spelling and social studies books and a wad of uncollected homework papers.

"Boy, it sure must have hurt a lot," George said. "You really acted brave, just getting up and walking off the court like that."

Peter practically had to crawl into his desk to find his math book, so George never heard whatever it was that he mumbled in reply.

At lunch time, George carried Peter's jacket and lunch bag for him, and stood in line an extra time to get him a carton of chocolate milk. He held the school door open so Peter could swing himself outside after lunch, and he even brushed the snow off a bench so Peter could sit down.

What a great friend, Peter kept thinking. *I wonder if he'd act this nice if he knew how I really hurt my ankle.*

"Now can I try them?" George asked.

"Sure," Peter said, sitting back and carefully lifting his injured leg up onto the bench. It still hurt if he bumped it. George took off across the snow, his red and black striped scarf flapping behind him. A few kids came over to ask if they could have a turn, too. Peter's basketball buddies wanted to know when he could play again. They seemed disappointed when Peter said, "Not till after Christmas."

"You know, we won on Saturday, by the skin of our teeth," one of Peter's teammates said. "Score was 21–19, too close for comfort. We could have used you."

Even Elizabeth came over to see how Peter was. She hadn't paid any attention to him in school since his first week of kindergarten, when she had given him a good, hard push each morning right into his classroom. She was mean and bossy then, and she seemed not to have changed for the better. "You'd better be careful with those crutches," she said now. "They don't belong to us, you know. If they get broken, you're really going to be in trouble."

"Mind your own business," Peter answered pleasantly. It was a nice day even though it was below freezing. The sky was a clear, dark blue, almost purple, and the sun shone so brightly off the snow that everyone had to squint. When George circled around, Peter got him to return the crutches. Peter broke open a fresh pack of bubble gum and offered a piece to George. The gum was so cold that it shattered instead of bending, but it tasted just as sweet as ever. Peter examined the new baseball card that came in the gum. Good. It was one he didn't have. He took his pile of cards out of his pocket and slipped the new one under the rubber band.

After a while, George asked, "Can you hold down the fort for a couple of minutes, ace? I'm going to shoot a few baskets, now that the court is shoveled."

For the first time all day, Peter was alone. He began to feel cold. He shoved his hands into his pockets, but there was nothing he could do to warm the foot that had two wool socks on it but no boot. He wished the bell would ring.

Then suddenly, despite the cold, Peter felt sweat break out under his arms. Sauntering toward him were the three biggest troublemakers in the whole school. Peter looked around. Maybe they weren't coming over to bother him. But a moment later they were looming over him, and there was no way to escape.

"What d'ya need these toothpicks for?" asked Dalton, the biggest of the three. He picked up one of the crutches that George had left lying on the bench.

Peter said nothing.

"I *said*, 'What d'ya need these toothpicks for?' " Dalton repeated, lowering his face until it was even with Peter's.

"Hurt my leg," Peter muttered.

"That a fact," Dalton said, inspecting the crutch. He passed it to the boy in a black leather jacket who was standing next to him. Peter put his hand on his other crutch, but Dalton lifted it out of his reach.

"Aw, ain't that a shame," the kid in the leather jacket said. The three of them clicked their tongues in mock sympathy.

"We didn't know things was so tough in fairyland," Dalton said. The other two laughed. Then they moved off, throwing the crutches into a bank of snowy bushes.

Peter sat trembling, his face burning against the cold air. "Fairyland . . . fairyland . . . fairyland . . ." echoed through his head. That was the scene he'd been dreading ever since he'd started ballet. Now it had happened. He thought he was going to throw up.

The bell rang, startling him. George came over to the bench. "Hey, what happened, ace?" he asked.

Peter told him, leaving out the part about fairyland. For all he knew, George really felt that way about ballet, too. George pulled the crutches out of the bushes and walked back into school next to Peter, holding open the heavy green door for him.

Who told them? Peter kept asking himself in class all afternoon. *Does everyone in the whole school know?* He felt carsick, even though he wasn't in a car. He wished he could lie down in the nurse's office, with its cool, green walls and half-drawn window shades, and bury his face in the smooth, soft, white pillow. He started to raise his hand to tell his teacher that he felt sick, but the thought of having to stand up and walk to the door in front of the whole class made him decide not to. Everyone would notice him, and then they would all talk about him after he'd left the room. He wondered if the kids at the back table, who were talking quietly as they worked on a science project, were talking about him. Were they laughing at him, a boy who does ballet dancing?

I've just got to get out of here. I've got to get home, Peter thought. But when the dismissal bell finally rang, he felt glued to his seat. He was afraid. Everyone would be waiting to get him when he went outside. Even George had left in a hurry. Peter's teacher stood by the door with her coat on, jangling her keys, waiting for him to hurry up so she could lock the door. Peter hung his book bag around his neck, leaving his hands free for his crutches. Slowly, he went outside into the glaring sunlight.

"Hey, Peter! Over here!" It was Elizabeth yelling.

Then he remembered. He couldn't go home after school. Even though he couldn't dance, he had planned to be at the ballet rehearsal from 3:30 in the afternoon until 10:00 at night. Sharon's mother was supposed to drive him and the two girls. As he made his way carefully over the hard-packed snow in front of the school to wait for his ride to the playhouse, a snowball grazed his shoulder.

"Hey, Peter. Over here," someone behind him called, mimicking Elizabeth's voice.

As he turned around, someone called from another direction, "Hey, Peter-boy, over here." A snowball hit him from behind, squarely between the shoulders. Then another hit him in the head.

"Okay, you guys," Peter said. "Cut it out." After all, the school yard was crowded, and snowballs were flying everywhere. Maybe the ones that hit him were nothing special. He stuck one of his crutches into the snow and bent down to gather up snow for a snowball. He didn't know whom to throw it at, but he stood ready, packing it firmly in the palm of his leather glove.

"Over here, ballet boy," someone yelled. Peter recognized Dalton's voice. Then the snowballs flew from all sides, and Peter knew they were for him. A crowd quickly gathered and formed a large circle around him. "Peter is a pansy," someone yelled. "Peter is a pansy," they chanted. "Dance, fairy, dance."

Peter threw his snowball with all his might, then bent over to gather snow for another. His book bag was heavy around his neck, and when he put his injured leg down to keep himself from falling over, the sudden pain in his ankle shocked him.

Where's everybody I know? he asked himself in despair as the nightmare closed in on him. He saw a sea of strange faces hidden in hoods, scarves, and ski masks. *Don't I have a single friend?*

"Shut up, you bullies," screamed a voice right behind Peter. "Just shut up!"

It was Elizabeth. Peter turned and saw her throw one snowball and quickly scoop up snow for another. "Why don't you pick on someone your own size?" she yelled. "Someone who isn't practically crippled. Or are you too chicken?" Her face red with rage, she slammed out the snowballs, throwing overhand with a furious energy. "You're the ones who are the sissies!"

Peter threw his book bag to the ground and began to pack snowballs and hurl them wildly in all directions. He felt no pain in his ankle now, and he didn't seem to notice the balls that hit him. "I'm a boy who dances," he said behind clenched teeth as he packed his snowballs. "But I'm *not* a fairy," he yelled as he fired them off. Over and over, like a machine, he packed and threw his snowballs.

"Hey, let the girls alone," someone finally said.

"Yeah," someone else said, "we don't fight with girls. Come on, let's let the girls alone."

A few more snowballs plopped harmlessly near Peter's feet, then it was all over. The kids who had gathered to watch the fight quickly drifted away. Peter noticed that George was one of them.

"Are you okay?" Elizabeth asked Peter.

"Sure," Peter said, his voice trembling, as he stooped to pick up his book bag. His ankle throbbed again, and so did his forehead, where an iceball had hit him. He took off his gloves, and with his fingers he scraped the snow off of his face and hair and out of his sleeves.

"We showed them," Elizabeth said proudly.

"Yeah, we showed them," Peter echoed in a small, pinched voice. He knew that if he talked any more he would start to cry. He vowed to himself never to come back to school again.

Sharon was calling to them, "Hurry up, my mother's here."

"Some friend you are," Elizabeth said to Sharon. "Why didn't you help us?"

"I don't know what you're talking about," Sharon answered. "Brush yourselves off. My mother doesn't like snow in the car."

"How could you *not* know what we're talking about?" Peter asked. Then, all of a sudden, he knew. It was Sharon who told the kids at school that he danced. He was sure of it! He could tell by the way she was smiling. *Elizabeth might be mean and bossy sometimes,* he thought, *but she would never try to ruin my whole life.*

"You know she's sleeping at my house," Sharon was saying. "The Sugar Plum Fairy, in person, is actually sleeping at my house. That's because my mother used to be a dancer. She arranged everything."

"Stop trying to change the subject," Elizabeth said as Sharon's old Chevrolet pulled up to the curb. "Are you a friend or not?"

Sharon ignored her and got into the back seat first. Elizabeth got in next, and Peter was still struggling with his crutches and the door when Sharon's mother introduced the woman who was sitting next to her on the front seat.

"This is Natalie Roberge," she said, beaming and flashing her red, lipsticked smile. *The* Natalie Roberge. Miss Roberge, I'd like you to meet my daughter, Sharon. You'll see her dance in the second act. She has been dancing since she was four. I didn't want to start her too young, but when a child shows such a strong interest at such an early age, and has such a beautiful body besides . . ."

Natalie Roberge nodded in the direction of the back seat. Sharon's mother didn't even give her a chance to smile and say hello. And although Sharon's mother didn't stop talking for one second, she never got around to introducing Peter and Elizabeth.

"How's your head?" Elizabeth asked Peter.

Peter gingerly felt his forehead, where a lump was rising. "Not so good," he said.

"You poor kid," Elizabeth said. "Well, at least you can bet Dalton feels worse."

"What do you mean?" Peter asked.

"His cheek. Boy, you almost smashed his whole face in."

"I did?" Peter asked in surprise.

"It wasn't me, so it must have been you," Elizabeth said. "There was no one else on our side."

"That's for sure," Peter said grimly, but he was beginning to feel better already. "I really got him, huh? I was throwing so hard and fast that I didn't have time to watch them land. I thought the whole school—the whole world—was out to kill me."

"It wasn't really that bad," Elizabeth said. "It was really just Dalton and his gang who were doing the throwing. Everyone else was just standing around watching."

"Yeah. Watching me get creamed. Who'd want to stick up for a fairy?" Peter said scornfully.

"He always makes such a fuss over everything, doesn't he?" Sharon said, trying to get Elizabeth's attention.

"You should talk," Peter said angrily. "It was all your fault in the first place. If it hadn't been for you—"

He was interrupted by Sharon's mother. "No fighting, Peter! Do you want me to stop the car and make you get out and walk?" Then she turned to Natalie Roberge and said, "That's boys for you. They're so loud and rough. I don't know why they can't keep out of things like ballet."

Natalie Roberge looked as though she were about to say something, but then she thought better of it and didn't. Peter thought that if he didn't know that she was a famous ballerina, he might think she was a boy herself. Her black hair was cut short, shorter than his own. She wore no makeup; her skin was pale, olive-toned, and her lips were almost the same color. Only her eyes, which were very dark and underscored by faint half-moons, looked like those of a grown-up woman.

I thought the Sugar Plum Fairy was supposed to be some kind of glamorous star, Peter thought. *I can't believe I've gone through all this to be in a show with the world's ugliest Sugar Plum Fairy. I should have stuck to basketball.*

When they arrived at the playhouse, Natalie Roberge opened her door immediately and got out. She leaned into the car and said to Sharon's mother, "You are most kind." Her English was so heavily accented that it sounded almost like a foreign language. Then she said to the children, "I am pleased to have met you," as though she wouldn't be seeing them again. By the time Peter had struggled out of the car with his crutches, Sharon and Elizabeth were already arguing loudly as they walked toward the playhouse, but Miss Roberge was still standing on the icy walk. She was waiting for Peter.

"Come," she said. "You must show me where is the stage door." She smiled at him, and for just a moment she looked like the beautiful ballerina in the glossy photos that were tacked to the ballet school bulletin board. If not for his crutches, Peter would have offered to carry her battered blue suitcase and bulging canvas bag for her. She looked small and very tired, standing there in her bulky tweed coat and heavy, flat-heeled hiking boots. *She's hardly taller than I am,* Peter realized in amazement as they skirted the icy patches on the walk and made it safely to the stage door.

Mr. Corbin was there, waiting for Natalie Roberge. While Peter fumbled in his pockets for his ID card to show the man on the stool, Mr. Corbin greeted Miss Roberge warmly with a kiss on each cheek. They seemed to be old friends. As Mr. Corbin ushered her upstairs, she turned and smiled again at Peter. "See you later, yes?" she said.

Peter was still slowly easing himself down the narrow staircase to his dressing room when Mr. Corbin came up behind him.

"So, today was the day they got you," he said. Peter turned in surprise. "Well, Peter, join the club. It happens to all of us. What did they do?"

"It was the crutches," Peter said. "That's how they found out." He decided it would be babyish to tattle on Sharon.

"But they would have found out anyway, sooner or later," Mr. Corbin said.

"I guess I thought I could always get away with it," Peter said. "I got by another whole year going to ballet class, and I didn't get caught on Saturday when I cut rehearsal for a little while so I could be in a basketball game." He hadn't meant to say that, but Mr. Corbin didn't seem to notice. "I was almost home free with only two more days of school left before vacation, but then it had to happen. I guess it was really because of basketball. I twisted my ankle at the game, and then I didn't have time to warm up before starting to dance Saturday afternoon. That's probably why I hurt my ankle so badly."

"What happened today?" Mr. Corbin asked. "Did they try to beat you up?"

Peter nodded. "First they took my crutches, then they threw snowballs."

Mr. Corbin gently touched the lump on Peter's forehead.

"But at least I got one of them back," Peter added proudly.

"I bet the names they called you hurt even worse than this bump," Mr. Corbin said.

Peter felt his face flush as he remembered the terrible words. How did Mr. Corbin know all this?

Mr. Corbin sat down on the stairs and put his arm around Peter's shoulders. He smiled sadly. "I remember when a similar thing happened to me," he said. "And I didn't even have the guts to fight back. But I learned, after a while." He sighed. "You know, some men just can't take it, and they quit dancing. Others carry their hurt around with them all the time—the ones who seem to have a chip on their shoulder. We have one of that kind right here in this show, and he's always giving me an argument over every little thing. Nothing is good enough for him—his contract, his dressing room, his rehearsal time. But some men just learn to live with it. You'll see."

Mr. Corbin patted Peter on the shoulder, then stood up. "Dr. Shultz tells me that you'll be good as new by Christmas," he said. "I know it's a tough break for you to go through all this and not even be able to dance at the opening, but the first time you dance will be your own private opening. Meanwhile, I want you to follow all the rehearsals, just as though you were going to be in every performance. I want to see you right at the edge of the wings, dancing through your part in your head. I don't want you to miss a single instruction. Okay, pal? Henry Reiff will fill in for you. He'll need a lot of coaching, and you can help. It's still your part, and I'm expecting great things of you. Remember that, okay?"

Mr. Corbin looked seriously into Peter's eyes. Only when Peter smiled at the unexpected gift of praise did he smile, too. "See you on stage, Peter," Mr. Corbin said.

Ten

After Mr. Corbin left him, Peter continued down the stairs to his dressing room.

"Hey, Peter's here," someone called as soon as he reached the door. He heard his name travel the length of the room.

"Come here, Peter," John called, making room for him to lean his crutches against the counter and sit down. "How's your ankle? Does it still hurt?" John asked.

"Ooooh, crutches!" Philip said. "Are those real crutches? Can I try them?"

Peter grabbed them just in time. "No you don't," he said. "You're too little."

"I am not!" Philip said.

"You are, too," Peter said. "These are taller than you are. They have to fit under your arms, see?" He showed Philip how they worked.

"Mommy," Philip whined, returning to his place, "can I have some crutches, too? Peter has them. Why can't I?"

Peter felt like a traveler arriving home safely after a long and dangerous trip. Here his crutches made him a celebrity, not a freak, like at school.

"What happened to your forehead?" John asked.

"Got hit by a snowball," Peter answered. "There was a big fight after school. You wouldn't believe what happened."

"Maybe I would," John said quietly.

"But I know whose fault it was," Peter continued, "and I'm going to get her, but good!"

He was interrupted by Mr. Corbin's voice coming from the intercom. "Attention, please. May I have your attention, please?" Everyone looked up at the speaker in surprise, for mixed with the usual static were the sounds of a live orchestra tuning up. Snatches of *Nutcracker* music floated behind Mr. Corbin's voice. "Will everyone in Act I, scene 1 report to the stage in five minutes? Act I, scene 1. Everyone else is welcome to watch from the house seats."

"Hey, Peter, you're going to have to tell me exactly what to do." It was Henry, the understudy. He was wearing Peter's dark blue velvet jacket. Fortunately, Henry was one of those boys who grow in sections instead of all at once. Although his legs were several inches longer than Peter's, and Mrs. DeRobertas had to find another pair of trousers for him, the upper part of his body was still almost the same size as Peter's. They just pulled his lace cuffs out a little to cover his bony wrists.

"Don't worry," Peter said. "I'll be right there for all the rehearsals. And you were in this scene last year, right?" Henry nodded. "It'll all come back to you."

"Who's your partner?" Henry asked.

"Lisa," Peter answered.

"Is she any good?" Henry asked.

"She's okay," Peter said, trying to sound casual. He wasn't at all pleased at the thought of Lisa dancing with Henry. He hoped she wouldn't get to like dancing with Henry better than she liked dancing with him.

"What does she look like?" Henry wanted to know. "Is she the short—"

"What difference does it make?" Peter interrupted. "You don't dance with partners right at the beginning anyway. Come on, let's go."

The orchestra had just finished the overture when the children for the first scene arrived on stage. The musicians were tuning and testing their instruments. A confusion of trills, tinkles, toots, and booms rose from the orchestra pit in front of the stage. It was the perfect accompaniment to the confusion on the stage. Adult dancers in full costume or parts of costumes, in practice clothes, and in street clothes crowded the stage. Some were just standing around talking. Others were finishing their warm-up exercises or trying out difficult steps.

In the midst of the chaos stood Mr. Corbin, listening to five people talk at once. He was running his hand through his hair, but he looked amazingly calm.

"Okay. Quiet," he called.

He shooed everyone who wasn't in the opening of the first scene off the stage and directed the children to take their places. Peter stayed on stage, next to Henry. Then Mr. Corbin introduced the conductor.

"This is Mr. Stefan Green," he said. "He's your commander-in-chief. Follow him, or you're lost."

Mr. Green was a large, balding man with gold-rimmed glasses. He wore a "Beethoven" sweat shirt, baggy brown pants, and sneakers. He looked rumpled and hot, although the rehearsal had just begun.

"Do you think he'll dress up and look like a real conductor for the performances?" Peter whispered to Henry.

"Sure," Henry said. "You'll hardly recognize him. You won't recognize the music, either. It sounds so different live than it did on the tape."

"Doesn't it make you feel important to have all those musicians playing for us to dance to?" Peter said.

"Shhh," Henry said. "Better get out of the way. He's starting."

Mr. Green tapped his baton on his metal music stand. There was a brief silence, then the music began. It was startlingly loud and bright. The rhythm was so exciting that it was impossible to hear it and not want to dance. Peter heard himself groan. He felt trapped by his crutches at the edge of the stage.

"Cut! Cut!" called Mr. Corbin almost immediately. "It would look a lot better if you all started at the same time. You can't just listen—you have to watch Mr. Green, too. Take it from the beginning. A little slower, Stefan."

This time the children watched intently as Mr. Green very deliberately indicated the tempo with his baton. He seemed to look everyone, musicians and dancers, in the eye. He gave the upbeat with his baton, and with an extravagant nod of his head, he led everyone in on the downbeat. Mr. Corbin smiled his approval.

They had to stop and start innumerable times as Mr. Corbin and the conductor set the tempo for each section. During the pauses, Peter coached Henry in his part. To Peter's relief, Lisa seemed much more interested in his injury than she did in Henry.

"I didn't know it was so bad you'd need crutches," she said. "And what happened to your head?"

"Oh, that's nothing," Peter said, smiling modestly. "Just a little fight at school. Come on, Henry. You're supposed to act as though you're having fun at a Christmas party." Peter thought he sounded a little like Mr. Corbin as he instructed and encouraged Henry. Once his memory was refreshed, Henry did very well. The ballet itself was the same from year to year; only the people performing it changed.

The rehearsal dragged on. It didn't seem possible that they would be ready, with only four more days to rehearse before the Saturday opening.

"I'm bored to death," Philip announced.

"And I'm scared to death," said Elizabeth.

Everyone in their group laughed, but they all agreed that they were bored and scared at the same time. And exhausted. When the first scene was finally finished, they straggled into the house, flipped down the bottoms of the plush maroon seats, and collapsed into them. From his seat, Peter searched the theater for Sharon, but he didn't see her anywhere.

The second scene got off to the same erratic start as the first. The mechanical Christmas tree grew toward the ceiling with sudden jerks. The young soloist playing Clara seemed confused in the flickering lights.

"Don't cut your *jetés* too short, honey," Mr. Corbin called to her. "You have a big stage to cover."

"Go from letter J," directed Mr. Green.

Stray flakes of snow intended for the Snow Forest scene drifted lazily through the glare of the overhead lights. The battle between the soldiers and the mice raged beneath.

"Sorry, Johnny. I cheated you out of a measure," Mr. Green said to the drummer, rapping his music stand for silence. The harried drummer, who had to create the sounds of battle on the kettledrums, a snare drum, and the cymbals, looked relieved at this news. They tried it again.

"Got it all?" Mr. Corbin asked at last.

Mr. Green nodded. He took off his glasses and wiped his sweaty face on his shirt sleeve.

"Okay. That's it for the Act I children," Mr. Corbin called out. "Go get something to eat, and be back here in an hour and a half. I don't know if we'll get to you again tonight or not, but I want you here. Act II children, you'd better eat right now, too, and be back by seven. Here we go with the Snow Forest scene."

"What do you want to do, Peter?" asked Elizabeth.

"Eat," Peter said. "I'm starved. I could use about three hamburgers and some French fries and—"

"Should I get yours to go, or do you want to come with me and Sharon?" Elizabeth asked.

"I'm coming," Peter said.

"Okay," said Elizabeth. "Get your coat. We'll meet you by the door."

When Peter got back up to the stage door, Elizabeth was already there. With her was a clown wearing Sharon's unmistakable white jacket with its fur-edged hood. The clown's face was chalk white, with eyebrows like little black roofs and pink circles painted on its cheeks. A thick, red smile extended beyond the ends of its real mouth, making it hard to tell if it was really smiling or not.

"How come you're wearing your makeup outside?" Peter asked. "Didn't anybody ever tell you that's unprofessional?"

"Oh," said Sharon lightly, "I forgot I had it on."

"How could you forget?" asked Elizabeth.

"She forgot," Peter muttered to himself. "What a phony! She's probably wearing it just to show off to the whole world that she's in the *Nutcracker*. But she won't be showing off by the time I'm done with her."

They had to walk single file all the way to the luncheonette because the path that had been shoveled through the snow was so narrow.

"Oh, no," said Elizabeth when they got there. A yellow sign hung in the window: "Closed Mondays."

Fortunately, the pizza place just a few doors down was open. A group from the ballet was already there. They waved and called hello. The jukebox was blaring, and a noisy game of pinball was going on in the back of the restaurant. Elizabeth ordered a large pizza for the three of them, half extra cheese and half sausage, and three root beers. They sat down at a table by themselves to wait until it was ready.

"Okay," Peter said, looking straight at Sharon. "Why did you do it?"

"I don't know what you're talking about," Sharon answered casually. She pulled three napkins out of the chrome napkin dispenser, folded them neatly, and placed one in front of Peter, one in front of Elizabeth, and one in front of herself.

"You do so," Peter said. "You told everyone at school that I'm taking ballet, and you tried to ruin my whole life."

"I did not," Sharon said. "I didn't tell *everybody,* and I didn't ruin your whole life. So there."

"You're a liar," Peter said, crumpling his napkin and throwing it at the table.

"Well, you must have told someone," Elizabeth joined in. "Why did you do it?"

"If you must know," Sharon said in a prim voice, "I was just talking to some of the kids about the Sugar Plum Fairy. I was telling them that she's so beautiful and famous, and that she's staying at my house because my mother used to be a famous dancer, too. They thought I was kidding—I could tell they didn't believe me. So I said they should ask you, Elizabeth."

"You're lying," Peter said. He was nearly shouting. People at the next table turned to see what was going on.

"I am *not* lying," Sharon said. "I don't lie."

"You do too," Elizabeth said. "That's the worst thing about you. Can't you ever admit it when you've done something wrong?"

Sharon looked from Peter's angry face to Elizabeth's, then down at the table. Her nervous fingers had shredded her napkin into dozens of little scraps. She brushed them off the table. Without looking up, she said, "Well, I might have said they should ask you *or* Peter. I really didn't mean to say 'Peter'—it just sort of slipped out."

"That figures," Peter said. "You were so busy showing off, just like your mother, that it 'just sort of slipped out' and you ruined my whole life. Now I can never go back to school again, and it's all your fault."

"Peter," Elizabeth interrupted, "you shouldn't talk nasty about people's mothers."

"Mind your own business," Peter said. "Whose side are you on, anyway?"

Just then the pizza was brought to their table. Peter helped himself to the slice with the most pieces of sausage on it, burning his fingertips in his hurry to be first. He chomped off as big a bite as his mouth could hold, not even caring that he was burning his tongue. He felt like taking a chomp out of Sharon.

"Did anybody ever tell you that you're a pig?" Sharon asked.

"Did anyone ever tell you that you're a phony?" He took another bite, as large as the first, and chewed it with his mouth open.

For a moment no one talked.

"Actually, Peter," Elizabeth finally said, "it was just a matter of time until the kids at school found out that you dance. You couldn't expect it to stay a secret forever, especially once you start performing."

"Yes," Sharon said. "And anyway, you ought to be able to take it."

"And if you can't take it, then you shouldn't have started dancing in the first place," Elizabeth added. Even though she was agreeing with Sharon, Peter could tell that Elizabeth was trying to be nice. She put the pieces of sausage that fell off of her pizza onto his plate. Peter felt better as the food in his stomach began to calm him.

"Just one snowball fight doesn't mean your whole life is ruined," Elizabeth continued, "though I wouldn't want to go through one like *that* again anytime soon."

"Like tomorrow," Peter said bitterly. "Well, thanks for standing by me, Lizzie," he said. "I only wish I'd seen the damage I did to Dalton's ugly face. At least we aren't cowards like *some* people we know." He looked right at Sharon.

Her painted smile was smearing and wearing off. Underneath, she looked quite miserable. "Don't you hate me, too," she said to Elizabeth.

"Well, why do you have to show off all the time?" Elizabeth asked her.

"I don't mean to," Sharon said, starting to shred another napkin. "In a way, you're right about my mother, though. She *is* always showing off and pushing me to be the best at whatever she wants me to do. Like ballet. She was so disappointed—actually she was angry—that I didn't get as good a part as you two did that I began to hate you. I know you deserved good parts. You both dance better than I do, even though I've been taking lessons longer than you, Peter. I know I'm not really any good at all. I'm not any good at anything. I don't know why I bother, except that . . . my mother makes me." She looked as though she were going to cry.

Peter patted his stomach and belched with satisfaction.

"I know what we need," Elizabeth announced brightly. "Hot fudge sundaes. Come on. Let's pay for the pizza and go."

At a little ice cream shop on the corner they ordered three hot fudge sundaes to go, with whipped cream and cherries. Peter couldn't manage his sundae and the crutches at the same time, so Elizabeth carried his cup and her own and fed him with the little plastic spoon. The fudge sauce lasted until the last spoonful of ice cream was gone.

"Isn't it great to be out at night without your mother hanging around?" Sharon said.

The night was so cold that very few people were out except for the dancers. As they squeezed past each other on the narrow side-walk, a kind of electric excitement passed between them. "Hi," everyone said to everyone else. It didn't seem to matter who was a grownup and who was a kid, who was famous and who was just a beginner. Their voices rang like music in the still, frigid air. The night sky was so clear that the stars seemed hung by strings, just out of reach, like Christmas lights in the tree branches.

"Hurry up," Elizabeth said. "We don't want to miss anything. We'll get to see our Sugar Plum Fairy dance tonight. I wonder why Mr. Corbin got such a funny-looking little fairy."

"Maybe all the good-looking ones were busy already," Sharon said. "Or maybe she was the best he could afford."

"She'll be okay," Peter said, remembering Miss Roberge's smile. "Anyway, maybe she can dance."

When they returned to their front row seats at the playhouse, the Sugar Plum Fairy and her partner, the Cavalier, were rehearsing their *pas de deux* from the end of Act II. Natalie Roberge looked even more boyish than she had in the car. Her body was stocky and athletic, with broad shoulders and protruding shoulder blades. Her legs seemed heavy in her thick, nubby, pink wool leg warmers.

"Anyone who would wear toe shoes so dirty you can't even tell what color they used to be can't be much of a ballerina," Elizabeth whispered to Sharon as they sat down.

"Shhh," Peter said.

Natalie Roberge seemed completely at home on the stage, and unaware that almost everyone in the ballet had come into the house to watch her. While talking animatedly with her partner and Mr. Corbin, she bent over and absentmindedly scratched her ankle. Then she pressed her elbows against her sides and wiggled her body until the bodice of her tutu was pulled up and properly centered on her bony chest. Satisfied, she fluffed out the stiff, dirtyish gray net of her short skirt. She fished a much-used tissue out of her bodice and blew her nose loudly. She sounded as though she had a cold.

"Ready?" called Mr. Green from the orchestra pit in front of the stage. "Here's the pickup."

Peter stared in astonishment at the transformation that suddenly occurred on stage. The Cavalier, who a moment before had looked more like a tennis player than a ballet dancer, with his white head band, T-shirt and socks, and his sinewy, muscular arms, now stood poised, body erect and head high, like a prince. And Natalie Roberge, by straightening her back, lowering her shoulders, and raising her chest, seemed to acquire a perfect dancer's body as if by magic. Her small head appeared delicately poised on a long, graceful neck, though a moment before she had barely any neck at all. Even her legs suddenly looked several inches longer as she pointed one foot, ready to begin. There was absolute silence.

On the downbeat, the Sugar Plum Fairy and the Cavalier took off in unison, as one person. Their dancing seemed completely natural, as though they knew no other way to move. One position flowed into another as easily as one breath leads to the next. They seemed to melt into the music, yet at the same time the positions of their feet were as neat and clean as if they were holding onto a *barre*.

"Can you believe it?" Elizabeth whispered to Peter.

"Wow!" was all he could say.

Natalie Roberge jumped straight up, her legs together. Her partner caught her, and as he did, she swung forward, back arched, arms outstretched, her feet pointing at the ceiling. She looked like a great swooping bird. Suddenly, she shot one arm forward, and the palm of her hand smacked against the floor. She had caught herself just in time. An instant later it would have been her chin instead of her hand that hit the floor.

The Cavalier dropped her in a heap. "Damn!" everyone heard him say. He spun around on his heels and walked toward the back of the stage, wiping his forehead on a towel draped around his neck. Mr. Green rapped his baton against his music stand, and the music faded away. Natalie Roberge sat on the stage, laughing and trying to catch her breath at the same time. Peter and Elizabeth smiled at each other with relief and settled back into their seats.

After a moment, Miss Roberge stood up, and hitching her thumbs under the thin shoulder straps of her tutu, she walked heavily to the front of the stage.

"Too slow," she said to the conductor. "A leetle beet too slow."

Mr. Green nodded and made a penciled note on his score. "Take it again from letter T," he said, and he hummed a few bars of the music to give the orchestra the new tempo.

The Sugar Plum Fairy and the Cavalier rejoined each other on stage. The Cavalier wiped his dripping face and neck again. This time, when the Sugar Plum Fairy swooped into her great arc, the

Cavalier let go of her, and she seemed to hang, miraculously suspended, inches above the floor. She broke into a dazzling smile, stood up, and kissed the Cavalier. The audience clapped and whistled.

"What do you think of that?" It was Mr. Corbin, who had sat down in the front row next to Peter without Peter noticing.

"I hate kissing," Peter replied. "But how does he do that? He *must* be holding her up somehow, and she must be pretty heavy, but he does it no hands."

"That's called a fish-dive lift. You can't see how it's done because her tutu is in the way, but she's balanced across his knee with her legs hooked under his arm when he lets go. Poor guy. He has to smile as though it's nothing while his back is killing him from playing catch with a full-grown woman. It's a very tricky lift. Maybe you'll learn it someday. Hey, do you hear that?" A clear, bell-like sound rose from the orchestra pit. Peter leaned forward to see what it was.

"That's the celesta," Mr. Corbin said. "Stefan plays it himself. He's just fooling around with it now. He's crazy about the sound."

"It sounds like a xylophone, but more ripply," Peter said.

"It's heavenly, isn't it?" Mr. Corbin sighed. "That's why it's called a celesta—it makes celestial music. It caused quite a sensation when Tchaikovsky first used it in this ballet. It was a new instrument that he saw on a trip to Paris. He liked it so much that he had one shipped back to Russia so he could use it in the *Nutcracker* music."

"How does it work?" Peter asked.

"Like a piano, except that the little hammers inside hit steel plates instead of strings," Mr. Corbin said.

Peter stood up to get a better look at the celesta. When he sat down, Mr. Corbin was in the aisle again, directing the rehearsal. It seemed to go on forever, with an order known only to Mr. Corbin. Most of the children sat in the first few rows of seats doing homework on their laps or reading with their feet propped up on the seat in front of them, or just talking quietly. They were always aware of what was happening on stage.

After a while, Peter lost track of time. He felt as though he had lived at the theater all his life. No other world seemed real. He couldn't believe that it was still the same day as the day of the snowball fight. Only by touching the spot on his forehead, which was still tender, could he prove to himself that he had another life, too. He tried not to think about the next day.

"We've been sitting here for hours and hours," Sharon complained, "and we still haven't been called up to rehearse the finale."

"Who cares?" Peter said. "I could watch all night."

"Look at that!" Elizabeth exclaimed. "Whoever thinks women are the weaker sex ought to take a look at this."

She was watching Natalie Roberge, who was practicing *fouetté* turns on the stage during a break in the rehearsal.

". . . ten . . . eleven . . . twelve . . . thirteen . . ," Elizabeth counted the turns.

"How does she do that?" Peter asked. "What makes her keep spinning on her toe without pushing off again with her other foot?"

"See how she whips her other leg out to the side?" Elizabeth said, as she kept counting, ". . . nineteen . . . twenty . . . twenty-one . . . twenty-two . . . Look at her feet. They're like steel springs. She's *so* strong! No wonder her toe shoes look worn—"

"Hey, what's going on?" Peter interrupted.

As if on a silent signal, all the musicians were standing up. A violinist who was seated directly in front of Peter placed her violin in its velvet-lined case and loosened her bow. She stretched and rubbed her eyes. All the musicians were packing up their instruments.

"It must be ten o'clock," said John, leaning toward Peter from his seat in the second row. "It's only Monday night, and they don't want to start paying the musicians overtime yet."

"That's it for tonight, folks," announced Mr. Corbin from the stage. "Tomorrow I promise we'll get all the Act II people up here for the finale even if we have to stay all night. Only four more rehearsals to go. Get a good rest, everyone. I want you kids to sleep late tomorrow—that's why you've been excused from school. Be back here . . ."

"Excused from school?" Peter repeated in astonishment.

"Don't you remember?" Elizabeth said. "We don't have to go to school tomorrow or Wednesday. After that it's vacation anyway. You mean you forgot?"

"How could you forget?" Sharon asked. "That's the best part of being in the *Nutcracker*."

"For you, maybe," Peter said. "But I guess I was so excited about being in the show that I just forgot."

"Oh, you poor kid," Elizabeth said. "You mean you thought you were going to have to go right back to school tomorrow and face those horrible bullies?" Peter nodded. "No wonder you were so mad at Sharon," she said.

On the way home, Peter relaxed and curled up in the corner of the back seat, on the verge of sleep. He had survived the scene he had been dreading since he started ballet, and now he could avoid seeing anyone from school for the rest of the month—until next year, in fact. He wiggled his foot gently. His ankle hadn't quite stopped aching since the snowball fight. If only it would heal in time for the opening.

"Would you like a sweet?" Natalie Roberge asked, turning around and holding out a small brown paper bag.

Peter, Sharon, and Elizabeth each took a candy.

"Are they sugarplums?" Elizabeth asked.

The Sugar Plum Fairy just smiled. She had been transformed again, back to a plain, pale woman with a boyish haircut and a stuffy nose.

"The house is dark," Elizabeth said as she and Peter got out of the car. "Mom and Dad must be asleep already. Lucky I have my key."

"Good," Peter said. "I don't want to talk to anybody. I just want to go to sleep."

But before they were all the way up the porch steps, the downstairs hall light flashed on, and their mother opened the front door.

"Hi, kids!" she called. "We were just beginning to get worried about you." She looked closely at Peter. "What happened to your forehead?" she asked.

"What forehead?" Peter answered, knowing there was no way out. His father, who had been sprawled on the couch watching the news on television, got up and came into the front hall.

"He got into a fight," Elizabeth said. "You should have seen—"

"We had pizza for dinner, and hot fudge sundaes," Peter said, trying to change the subject. The last thing he needed was for Elizabeth to repeat in front of his father the names the kids had yelled at him. He and his father had barely spoken to each other since the ride home from Dr. Shultz's office.

"Maybe we'd better put some ice on that awful-looking bump on your head," Peter's mother said, "so it doesn't swell any more."

His father said, "He'll be all right. Leave him alone. Peter, what kind of fight did you get into?"

"Just a fight," Peter said, starting up the stairs. "I'm pooped. Don't wake me in the morning. We're excused from school, remember?"

"It was a horrible, terrible snowball fight," Elizabeth said. Peter sighed and sat down on the second step. "We were all alone," Elizabeth continued, her eyes shining. "It was just us against the whole school."

"Why did they pick on you two, of all people?" their mother asked.

Peter sighed again, and everyone looked at him. *Might as well*

100

get it over with, he thought. "The word got out that I dance," he said, "and, just like Dad said, it didn't exactly make me the most popular kid in the school."

"But boy, we showed them, didn't we?" Elizabeth said. "I was throwing those snowballs so hard and fast I didn't even have time to be scared!"

"I did," said Peter.

Elizabeth laughed. "Peter didn't even see one of his snowballs connect with Dalton's face. It's just lucky I happened to see it, or he wouldn't even have known that he did it. The fight was all over after that."

"Peter, how's your ankle?" his mother asked. "How could you fight with that sore ankle? Did you have to put your weight on it?"

"I guess I did," Peter answered. "It hurts a little now."

"Come up right now and soak it," his mother called back, as she and Elizabeth went upstairs.

"So you got Dalton?" his father asked. "You mean that great big kid who plays halfback—and the one I used to see playing basketball? He's older than you are, isn't he? Whatever happened to him? I haven't seen him at any games lately."

"He got kicked off the team," Peter answered. "He's tough, but the coach said he wasn't worth the trouble. He made more personal fouls than baskets. Coach says it takes discipline to play in a game, and Dalton didn't have it."

"And you put him out of action with a snowball today?" Peter's father asked with a smile he couldn't hide.

"I guess so," Peter answered.

"That's great," his father said.

"I guess so. I think I'll go to bed now."

"You know," said his father, sitting down on the step next to Peter, "you have a lot more guts than I gave you credit for."

Peter shrugged. "It's not exactly gutsy when you don't have any choice, is it? If I could have gotten out of that fight, I sure would have. Talk about guts—you should have seen Lizzie!"

"But you knew all along that something like this might happen if the kids found out that you dance, and you decided to be in the *Nutcracker* anyway," said his father. "Dancing must mean an awful lot to you."

"That's what I've been trying to tell you, Dad," Peter said quietly.

Peter's father stood up. "Let me turn out the lights down here," he said. "Then I'll help you up the stairs."

"I can manage by myself," Peter said. But his father's arm was steadier than the crutches, and it felt wonderful to lean his tired head against his father's chest.

Eleven

Saturday, December 20, the day of the opening performance, was a strange kind of day right from the start. Peter tried to sleep late because the final dress rehearsal the night before had run until eleven o'clock, but he was sweating just lying in bed. He got up and tested his ankle, as he did every morning. He felt no pain at all.

Taking his crutches anyway, Peter went downstairs and opened the front door. No wonder he was sweating; it was much too warm for a December day. A soft breeze, the kind that isn't supposed to come until March, blew against his face, bringing with it the smell of damp earth. Peter felt light-headed as he stood in the open doorway in his pajamas.

"Going somewhere?" his mother asked.

"You bet," Peter answered. "And without these stupid crutches. My ankle doesn't hurt at all any more. I'm sure it would be okay to dance on it today."

"Peter," his mother said, "you know that Dr. Shultz said you can't dance until the twenty-sixth. Mr. Corbin wouldn't let you disobey the doctor, would he?"

Peter scowled. "It wasn't so bad when we were just rehearsing," he said. "Then there was always a crowd sitting out front watching with me, so I didn't feel left out. But now I don't see how I'll be able to stand it. Everyone will be dancing but me. I think I'll just go back to bed."

"Don't do that," his mother said, stopping him. "Why don't you come to the theater with me and Dad to watch Elizabeth dance?"

"Are you kidding?" Peter asked. "The whole world will be there. Elizabeth has invited everyone she knows, which means every girl in the whole school. You've invited your twenty-five best friends. I'll bet Sharon's mother even invited her dentist and the mailman. No thanks. I don't want to see any of them, and I especially don't want them to see me. I'm going back to bed."

"Well, you do whatever you think best, dear," his mother said in her most reasonable voice. "I'm going to help Elizabeth get ready."

"Mom," Peter said, "I hate it when you let me decide things for myself. Why can't you nag and yell like mothers are supposed to? What's the matter with you, anyway? All right, maybe I will go to the playhouse with Lizzie. Mr. Corbin said he expects me to be backstage for every performance anyway."

Peter's mother hugged him. "I do my best for both my dancers," she said. They walked into the kitchen together, just in time to see Elizabeth slide into a split.

"Elizabeth!" Mrs. Harris yelled. "Are you crazy? You might pull a muscle or something." Then she caught herself and said calmly, "Of course, if you *want* to watch the ballet from the wings with Peter, then you can keep right on splitting. It's entirely up to you."

They all laughed, and Peter sat down to watch his mother take the curlers out of Elizabeth's hair and brush it into long corkscrew curls. Suddenly, she dropped one of the curlers. "What's this? Blood!"

"Oh, Mom," said Elizabeth. "It's just red nail polish that spilled on it. You're more nervous than I am."

"I'm not nervous," her mother said. "Anyway, it's good to be nervous before an opening."

"What's it good for, Mom?" Peter asked.

"It makes you try harder," his mother answered firmly. She pulled Elizabeth's hair back into a pony tail of shiny curls. "You look adorable," she cooed. "Absolutely precious." She picked up a tall blue can and started spraying Elizabeth's hair.

"I feel old," Elizabeth said, "like a real dancer. This is how the best girl in my group wears her hair . . . Mom, what's that funny smell?" They all sniffed and looked around.

"Oh, Mom!" wailed Elizabeth. "That's not the hair spray. That's starch you're spraying on my hair!"

They both laughed until they cried, and still they couldn't stop.

"I'm getting out of here," Peter said, "before something really happens." He went upstairs to get dressed.

It was stuffy in the car on the way to the theater. The smell of old cigarette ashes and used chewing gum rose from the ash trays.

"Open the window," Elizabeth said to Peter. "I think I'm catching your pre-ballet car sickness. I'm so nervous my teeth are shivering."

Standing outside of the playhouse, facing the street, was a large red and white sign. *The Nutcracker,* starring Natalie Roberge," it announced in bold letters. A strip of yellow paper was just being pasted diagonally across the poster. On it was printed "TODAY."

"Don't forget," said their mother as she let Elizabeth and Peter off in the parking lot, "Daddy and I will be sitting in row E, on the right. We'll meet you both at the stage door when it's over. Good luck, dear," she said, kissing Elizabeth.

"Don't say that, Mom," Peter said. "It's bad luck to say 'good luck' to a dancer. Now something terrible will probably happen to Elizabeth."

"That's just a silly superstition," Elizabeth said.

"You're supposed to say, 'Break a leg,' " said Peter. They looked at his crutches and laughed, but it didn't seem funny to Peter.

It was hot and even noisier than usual in the boys' dressing room. Most of the boys were already there when Peter arrived, doing their warm-up *pliés* and bending and stretching in time to the top ten tunes that blared from someone's portable radio.

"Hey," yelled little Philip, "every time I do an *échappé* my pants fall down!" Everyone laughed.

"No wonder," scolded his mother. "Those aren't your pants. Where did you get them?" She stood Philip on a chair and pulled his trousers off. "Who's missing a pair of size twelves?"

"Those must be mine," Peter said. He folded them neatly and hung them up on the empty costume rack. Then he stood for a long time looking out the window, watching the parking lot fill with cars. John came over to keep him company and did his *pliés* holding onto the windowsill.

"Just last year I was one of them instead of one of us," Peter said. "Life sure was easier then. Look how happy they are out there. They could be coming to see a movie, for all they know about what really goes on. They don't even know we're real, do they?"

"This is already my second year," John said. "I can hardly remember what it's like to be one of them. I guess you just get so used to it—the fun *and* all the other stuff you have to go through—that you can't imagine living any other way."

"Act I, scene 1—five minutes to curtain," called a voice from the hallway.

"Now look in the mirror, boys," directed Philip's mother. "Help each other. Check each other over. Be sure your hair is still combed."

"You look okay," Peter said to John, smoothing the shoulders of his velvet jacket.

"Come on," John said. "It's time to go right now."

The muffled sound of faraway applause, followed by the beginning of the overture, greeted the boys as they approached the backstage area. They pushed each other toward the stage, jumping and twitching like a bag full of Mexican jumping beans.

"Cool it, guys," said Mr. Corbin. "Just take your places. Quietly. Peter, you stand right here, so you can see everything but not be seen."

The girls were grimly silent as they arrived in the wings.

"I'm so scared I think I'm going to faint," Elizabeth whispered as she passed Peter.

Peter was going to say, "Oh, come on, you couldn't faint if you tried," but when he saw that the pale freckles on her nose were showing, he realized that she might be telling the truth. He touched her arm. "You'll knock 'em dead, Lizzie," he said. "Break a leg!"

That seemed to help. He heard her hiss at Philip, "Hey, watch it, buster. You're kicking me again." She brushed imaginary dirt off of her white ruffled pantaloons. The overture ended, and the applause was loud and very near.

"Okay, kiddos," said Mr. Corbin. "You're on. Break a leg!"

In the instant before the green velvet curtain rose, Peter caught Lisa's eye and smiled at her. She smiled back and was still smiling when the curtain went up. For better or worse, the enormous production was underway.

Alone in the dim light at the edge of the wings, Peter leaned on his crutches and squinted into the hot, brilliantly lit world on the stage. He watched his friends—John, Elizabeth, Lisa, Henry, Philip, and the others—pretend to be old-fashioned children at Clara and Fritz's Christmas party. They were playing blindman's bluff. It looked like a real game of pushing and chasing and groping around blindfolded, but Peter knew that it was all done according to plan and had been rehearsed exactly the same way dozens of times.

When the set opened to reveal the Christmas tree garlanded with twinkling lights, the audience clapped in appreciation. As the

"March" began, Peter's leg muscles twitched in their eagerness to dance. On stage, the dancing was good but not perfect; the boys in the center were bunched too close together. But it must have satisfied the audience because when the boys finished with their salute, the applause began with a sharp crack.

I hope they still feel like clapping when I'm out there dancing, Peter thought.

"Hey, man. Hey! Pete!" one of the stagehands whispered hoarsely. "Could you help us out for a minute?"

Peter followed the man into the shadowy area behind the stage.

"Listen," said the man. "We think this pulley is jammed. We want to test it before it's time for the tree to grow. I'm gonna pull the lever. I want you to tell me if this rope moves."

"Yes, sir," said Peter.

"Not 'yes sir,' " said the man. "The name is Freddy."

"Okay, Freddy," said Peter. "I'll watch it."

In a moment the rope quivered, and Peter reported back to Freddy.

"Whew!" said Freddy. "Thanks. Say, listen, Pete. Would you give us a hand with this here flat? Just hold this end steady."

Soon Freddy had Peter so busy helping backstage that he had no time to watch the performance. He was surprised when he saw Elizabeth and the other children backstage.

"I nearly died!" Elizabeth gasped. "Did you see me? I really nearly died."

"What happened?" Peter asked.

"Didn't you see? There wasn't any doll in my box!" she said breathlessly. "They passed out the Christmas presents, and we all opened them to take out the dolls, but my box was empty. I couldn't believe it!"

"What did you do?" Peter asked.

"I just pretended I had one," Elizabeth replied. "I did the whole lullaby waltz with a pretend doll in my arms."

"You handled it like a real pro," Mr. Corbin said, coming up behind them. "I bet no one but your parents noticed. If that's the worst that happens today, we're in good shape. Go wait quietly now for your curtain call."

Peter could tell that Elizabeth was enjoying the excitement, now that the shock was over. He could hear her telling everyone how she had "nearly died."

She probably thinks she upstaged Philip at the very least, thought Peter. *I'll bet she hopes her box will be empty at every performance.*

Toy soldiers and mice crowded the wings. The lights on stage were flickering. The battle was about to begin. Peter helped pass out plastic swords and rifles to the soldiers as they marched on stage. Now, as drums rolled and trumpets blared and red lights flashed across the darkened stage, Peter was amazed at how real the battle scene appeared. The Mouse King fell with a convincing thud, killed by Clara's slipper. In the sudden hush that followed, Peter heard a young child in the audience cry with fright. Freddy slapped the man in charge of lighting on the back to congratulate him. Then he turned to Peter and winked. Peter could see that Mr. Green was smiling, too, as he led the orchestra with sweeping gestures into the romantic music of Clara's duet with the Nutcracker Prince.

"Poor kid," Mr. Corbin said to Peter. "She's still scared to death of being dropped."

"I don't blame her," Peter whispered. "Look how his arms are shaking."

"That's because she doesn't jump enough. He has to heave her up onto his shoulders. But having perfect control isn't everything. Look at their line—that beautiful curve from his arm to her leg. He was our Fritz a few years ago, and now he's with a professional company. I bet she will be too, before long. The *Nutcracker* is just the beginning for one or two kids every year. Picking them and training them is half the fun for me."

A wave of applause washed onto the stage as the Prince gently lowered Clara onto her white bed. She looked more relaxed now, but Peter could see how white her knuckles were as she gripped the bed's headboard. The bed always jerked a little as it started to roll on its magic journey.

Dancers in long white tutus lined up backstage, ready to whirl across the stage like living snowflakes. The glittering Snow Forest backdrop was lowered into place, and a few stray flakes of fake snow drifted through the cool, blue lights.

"I wish I'd worn more deodorant," Peter overheard one dancer say to another as they waited near him for their musical cue. "It looks so cool, but it's always hotter than blazes out there."

The scene ended with a gentle snowfall of Styrofoam bits. Peter joined the men with wide brooms who began sweeping the stage clean the instant the curtain closed. He hardly noticed the children from scenes 1 and 2 as they lined up to take their curtain call. Act I was over.

During the intermission, two little blond boys in matching red sweaters and green overalls appeared backstage. Of everything there was to see, they seemed to find Peter's crutches the most fascinating of all. While their mother talked to Mr. Corbin, they held her hands and stared at Peter.

Mr. Corbin called Peter over. "These are my boys," he said, "Jonathan and Timothy. And my wife, Suzanne."

Mrs. Corbin was very pretty, with reddish-brown hair parted in the middle and pulled back like a dancer's. Peter wondered if she danced, too.

"Boys, would you like Peter to give you a guided tour back here?" Mr. Corbin asked. They nodded. "Just look," their father said in a stern voice that Peter had never heard him use before. "Don't touch."

The little boys shyly followed Peter through the backstage world. They touched everything they saw, from the candy-striped throne being rolled into place for Clara and the Nutcracker Prince, to the rosin box on the floor for the dancers to rub their shoes in to make them less slippery. When the younger boy bent over to pick up a strand of glitter that must have fallen from the Christmas tree and started to put it in his mouth, Peter said, in his most fatherly voice, "No, no, Jonathan. That's not for eating." He fished a candy cane he had been saving for himself out of his pants pocket and broke it in half, giving a piece to each little boy. "Are you going to be dancers like your daddy?" Peter asked them. Wide-eyed, and sticky already, they both nodded, then ran back to their mother. Peter saw them twirling around dizzily and imitating the march of the toy soldiers while they waited for the intermission to be over.

"There's nothing much to do now that the second act set is ready," Freddy said to Peter. "Why don't you find yourself an empty seat in the house so you can watch in comfort?"

Peter shook his head. *This is where I belong,* he thought. He heard the audience clapping. Mr. Green must have returned to the orchestra pit. The stage filled with dancers waiting to welcome Clara and the Nutcracker Prince to the Kingdom of Sweets. Natalie Roberge stood right beside Peter, but she didn't seem to see him. She rubbed her toes in the rosin box like a horse nervously pawing the ground. She checked the knots in her toe shoe ribbons, pushed in the hairpins which anchored her crown to her wig, checked both her earrings. Then she stood absolutely still, as though in a trance, waiting for her cue.

As the curtain rose, Peter's eyes were drawn to Mr. Green's face, which was glowing in the light from his music stand against the sea of darkness behind him. He looked tall and impressive in a black suit and bow tie. His gold-rimmed glasses sparkled as he swayed to the music. Peter noticed that when it was time for him to play the celesta, he conducted the orchestra by nodding his head to the beat. He smiled as he played, obviously delighted with the silvery, bell-like tones he was producing.

As he resumed conducting with his baton, a strange thing happened. He looked up and happened to catch Peter's eye. A sudden blush colored his face. Perhaps he was embarrassed at having been caught having such fun just making lovely sounds. Perhaps he thought it appeared undignified for a grownup to enjoy himself that much at his work. He quickly looked down at his music and pushed his glasses further up on his nose, half covering his face with his hand in an attempt to hide his embarrassment. Then, surprisingly, he glanced up at Peter again, and this time he smiled, letting Peter in on his private pleasure.

Peter felt something he had never felt before. It began as a warm glow of affection for the conductor. Then it quickly turned into an intense feeling that there was a secret bond of brotherhood between them. Suddenly, Peter understood that it was wonderful, that it was a rare and precious gift, for a person to get such pleasure from just making music. And for the first time in his life, Peter accepted his own love of dancing as that same kind of special gift.

He was filled with such an overwhelming feeling of warmth and light that he couldn't contain it. It seemed to radiate from him in concentric rings reaching beyond the footlights, beyond the last row of seats, beyond his world of family and friends, to the whole world, to the sky, to the entire universe. He felt so light he thought his body was floating above the floor and his mind was floating free of his body.

". . . stands here to make it work, okay? Or not? Can you tell?" Mr. Corbin was standing next to Peter, asking him something.

Peter blinked and shook his head, trying to pull the beginning of Mr. Corbin's sentence out of the air.

"Are you all right, Peter?" Mr. Corbin asked. "You look a little funny. You'd better sit down for a minute."

"I'm fine," replied Peter. "Really, I'm fine. I've never felt better in my life."

Mr. Corbin gave him a strange look, then left him alone. Peter didn't know what to do. He wondered if he were going crazy. All he knew was that he wanted to share his new feeling of freedom with someone he knew. He quickly left the backstage area and went down a long hallway to a double door through which he could hear clapping. He opened it and let himself into the theater. Maybe he could find an empty seat near his parents. In the semi-darkness, he thought he saw a familiar plaid shirt on someone sitting in an aisle seat, in the second to last row.

"George!" he said, as the applause for the Sugar Plum Fairy continued. "Is that you? What are you doing here?"

George jumped in his seat, then looked as though he wished a manhole would suddenly appear so he could drop into it.

"What does it look like I'm doing here?" he asked as Peter slipped into an empty seat behind him, in the last row. "I'm eating mints, that's what I'm doing, since they don't even have popcorn at this place."

"I mean," Peter whispered, "why did you come to see the *Nutcracker?* I didn't know you liked ballet."

"My grandmother made me come," George whispered back, nodding in the direction of a lady in a tall fur hat two seats over. "She wanted my little sister to see it, and she said it would do me good. I don't know what kind of good it could do me, but here I am."

"What do you think of it?" Peter asked him.

"Well, it's okay for little kids," George said offhandedly. A little girl with braids sitting next to George had turned around in her seat and was staring at Peter's crutches. "This is my sister," George said. "You should have seen her face when the Christmas tree started to grow."

"Was she the one who screamed during the battle scene?" Peter asked.

"Uh-uh," said George, shaking his head. "But she looked pretty scared."

"I did not," his sister said.

"We took her up to the front to see the drums during intermission," George continued, "so she'd know how they made all that noise. The drummer let her try the big ones."

"We have a great drummer," said Peter. "His name's Johnny. You should have seen him rehearsing that battle scene. He nearly went crazy."

"Hush!" said George's grandmother. George's sister turned

around and Peter moved over, making room for George to sit next to him.

"What do you mean, 'we'?" George asked. "Are you in this show?"

"You bet," Peter said proudly. "I'm just not dancing today because of my ankle. Didn't you see my name in the program?"

George looked both shocked and puzzled. "I didn't even know you took dancing lessons," he said, "until the snowball fight the other day. Then I wasn't sure if it was true or not. How come you never told me?" He sounded hurt. "I thought we were best friends."

"I said hush!" George's grandmother ordered, glaring at Peter.

"Tell you later," Peter whispered. "I want to watch this now."

In the darkness, the scene on the stage glowed like a small but brilliant jewel against a background of black velvet. The stage lights made everything appear unusually sharp and vivid, the way things look when seen through the wrong end of a telescope. Peter knew that the scenery was a flat set, with a gingerbread house, gum drops, and candy canes just painted on it. Yet from the back row, the illusion of sparkling crystals of sugar and soft, gooey icing was real enough to make his mouth water.

During the lilting "Waltz of the Flowers," Peter thought about the strange experience he had had backstage while watching Mr. Green play the celesta. He tried to make the weightless feeling return, but he couldn't. He wanted to tell George about it, but at the same time, he was afraid it might spoil it to talk about it. His ballet dancing had been a secret because he had been *afraid* to share it; this was a secret because he didn't *want* to share it. He decided to keep it to himself forever, or at least until he felt like telling someone, like Lisa—someone who would really understand.

Peter clapped enthusiastically for the waltzing flowers, and again when the Spanish dancers finished entertaining Clara and the Nutcracker Prince. Then, right in the middle of the Arabian dance, he started to clap again, even though no one else was applauding and the music hadn't stopped.

"Clap!" he ordered, giving George a sharp nudge with his elbow. "Do you think it's easy to turn like that in the air and land in a perfect fifth position? He just makes it *look* easy, which makes it even harder."

George gave three quiet little claps, then sank down into his seat. People turned around to see who was clapping out of turn, but Peter paid no attention.

"He's about 6'5" and he teaches judo and karate, too," Peter assured George. "I'll introduce you to him if you ever want to come backstage."

Peter continued to clap loudly at every opportunity. When the man dancing the Russian trepak did a series of splits in the air, with his hands touching his toes, Peter stood up and whistled. Everyone clapped so hard for the trepak that the last section of it was repeated as an encore. Peter looked as proud as if he had danced it himself.

When the clown children came tumbling out from under Mother Ginger's skirt, Peter whispered, "There's my sister's friend, Sharon. Third clown from the left. Watch her cartwheels."

As the Sugar Plum Fairy and the Cavalier began their *pas de deux*, Peter said to George, "I know her." Then he wondered if he did know her. Natalie Roberge, wearing a glittering short pink tutu and a sparkling crown, looked as dainty and beautiful as a fairy should. Peter knew that sweat was trickling down her costume and that her muscles were straining, but all he could see was her radiant smile and her precise and effortless-looking dancing. The illusion was perfect.

"She's wearing a wig," he informed George. "She really looks like a boy."

George thought Peter was kidding, so he laughed quietly.

"Hey, watch this," whispered Peter when the Sugar Plum

Fairy and the Cavalier began the preparation for their fish-dive lift. Peter sucked in his breath as Natalie Roberge swooped forward. She hung suspended, arms outstretched, inches above the floor, smiling triumphantly. Peter let his breath out with relief and clapped until his palms were numb.

"Just six more days and I'll be up there, too," he said as the curtain calls continued. "Do you think you could stand to see it again?" he asked George. "I'll be dancing in the three performances after Christmas. If you come, you could go backstage afterward and meet everyone, then come back to my house."

George looked uncomfortable. "Do you really want me to," he asked, "after what happened at school?"

"Forget it," Peter said. "It doesn't matter any more. Anyway, all the men here—even the director—go through that sort of thing sometime or other. You just have to be able to take it."

"We really could have used you at basketball this week," George continued. "No one's as good as you at grabbing those rebounds. No one else can jump up for them the way you can. You should have seen—"

He was interrupted by his grandmother. "Young man," she said to Peter, tapping him on the shoulder rather sharply with her rolled-up program. "Young man, since you are in fact a dancer, would you be so kind as to autograph my program? It would mean a great deal to my granddaughter, wouldn't it, Hillary? Stand up straight, Hillary. Haven't you learned anything at dancing school?"

Hillary hung onto her grandmother's hand and stared at Peter's crutches. Peter flipped through the program until he found the page where his name was listed. He signed with such a flourish that he couldn't even read it himself. He gave the program to Hillary, who was still staring at the crutches as her grandmother dragged her off. The little dead furry animals that were draped around her grandmother's shoulders glared back at Peter with their beady glass eyes.

"See you soon," George said, following his grandmother out of the theater.

"See you," Peter called happily, and he went to meet his parents at the stage door.

Twelve

Someone was pounding on the front door. "I'll get it," Peter called, jumping to his feet. It was the day after Christmas, and Peter finally was able to dance again. He stuffed his ballet shoes into his jacket pocket as he rushed to the door.

"It must be Sharon," he said to Elizabeth. "She's early. Come on. Let's go." He opened the door.

"Hi there, sports fans!" roared a big, familiar voice.

"Pearson!" said Peter in surprise.

"Who did you think it was? Santa Claus?" asked Bob Pearson as he stamped into the house. He shook himself like a dog to get the snow off his hair and shoulders.

"Mom! Dad! Pearson's here!" Peter yelled.

"Hi there, Elizabeth," said Pearson.

Elizabeth felt herself blush even before Pearson said, "You're looking prettier than ever."

"What are you doing here?" asked Peter, helping Pearson hang his coat up to dry.

"What am *I* doing here?" Pearson asked. "What are *you* doing here? I thought you were supposed to be at the theater already. I was going to surprise you after the show."

"You mean *you're* coming to see the *Nutcracker?*" Peter asked in amazement.

"Is that why you look so different today?" Elizabeth asked. "So fancy?"

Pearson inspected himself carefully in the hall mirror. Usually, he wore big, nubby sweaters and jeans or baggy corduroy pants that looked as though they were left over from his college days. Now he was all dressed up in a dark gray pin-striped suit with a matching vest, and a blue and green plaid tie. "Haven't you ever seen me in my grown-up costume before?" he asked seriously. He smoothed down his hair, which was damp from the snow. "You have to look proper to go to the ballet, right, ballerinas? What's the matter, Peter?" he asked, catching Peter's eye in the mirror.

"It's too bad you bothered to get so dressed up," Peter said, "because I don't think you're going to like it."

"Do you like it?" Pearson asked.

"I love it," Peter said, looking Pearson square in the eye. "I can hardly wait to get out there on that stage."

"Well," Pearson said, "if you love it, and your dad is so proud of you now that you're in the big leagues, working out with the pros—"

"Did he really say that?" Peter interrupted.

"He sure did," Pearson said, slapping Peter on the back. "Well, I guess it's about time I gave it a whirl myself. How do you know what you don't like until you try it, right, big-leaguer?"

Peter and Elizabeth's parents came downstairs and greeted Pearson warmly.

"Why don't you each invite a few friends over after the performance?" their mother said. "With Pearson here, we'll have a real party."

"Great!" said Peter. "Hey, I think I just heard a horn honking."

Elizabeth ran to the front window. "That really is Sharon this time," she called. "Come on, Peter. Let's go."

"Wait a minute," their mother said firmly. "Zip up. It's freezing out there. Be sure you have everything. Don't muss your hair, lovey," she said to Elizabeth, tying a silk scarf over her smoothly parted hair and curled pony tail. She kissed Elizabeth. "We'll be watching," she whispered to Peter. Then she kissed him on the forehead.

"Cut it out, Mom," he said, wiping the kiss off with the back of his hand.

"I'm afraid to say it," Peter's father said to him, glancing at the crutches leaning against the wall, "but break a leg, Peter. You too, honey," he said to Elizabeth.

"Why don't you let the poor kids go?" Pearson said. He opened the door, and Peter and Elizabeth dashed out into the silently swirling snow.

Once he was settled in the back seat of Sharon's car, Peter felt warm and safe, like a butterfly in a cocoon. He was certain that he would never again be bothered by car sickness while going to ballet. He wiggled his foot inside his boot; his ankle felt fine.

"I'll bet you're nervous, aren't you, Peter?" asked Sharon's mother, breaking in on his thoughts.

"A little, sure," answered Peter. "It's *good* to be nervous, though—it's stage energy. My mother told us that." The girls giggled. Even Sharon's mother couldn't annoy him today. "But anyway, I'm not really nervous," he added. "Just excited."

When they arrived at the playhouse, the three children ran through the snow from the parking lot toward the stage door. Suddenly, Peter stopped. He tilted his head back, shut his eyes, and opened his mouth.

"What's the matter?" called Elizabeth. "Hurry up!"

Peter didn't budge until he had savored the icy treats that fell out of the sky onto his tongue. Then he caught up with the girls as they opened the stage door.

"Never mind, never mind," said the man on the stool, as they fumbled in their pockets for their ID cards. He waved them on.

"See you on stage," Peter called. He headed downstairs to his dressing room. John was already there, wearing tights, T-shirt, and face makeup, when Peter arrived.

"Hey! I'm here!" Peter announced.

"Mm," said John. He tipped back in his chair, his feet on the counter. In front of him was an array of brand new comic books, spread out in a neat fan. He was deeply engrossed in a Captain Marvel comic.

Peter grabbed it out of his hands. "I'm here," Peter repeated. "I'm dancing. Today!"

"Great!" said John, retrieving his comic book. "Don't be scared. You'd be surprised how you can get used to it in just a few days."

"Not me," said Peter. "I'll bet I never get used to it."

"Go get yourself ready," John said. "Then you can look at my new comic books."

Peter found his dark blue velvet jacket hanging on the costume rack. Carefully, he took it down.

"Just the tights now," said Philip's mother, who was guarding the costumes. "Otherwise you'll have to stand up until curtain time to keep from wrinkling your clothes. Go get made up."

Peter stood in front of the makeup lady with his eyes shut. He felt a cold, slippery cream being smeared over his face, then a pull around his eyes as they were outlined with a greasy pencil. His eyebrows were penciled, too. Then his lips were touched with something sticky, and his whole face was dusted with powder. It made him sneeze.

"You can open your eyes now," the lady said.

Peter was startled by the face he saw in the mirror. He hardly recognized himself. His skin was a rosy tan, his mouth a dull, dark red and his eyes looked huge beneath long, dark brows.

Well, at least I don't look like a girl, he thought. *I hardly even look human.*

"Can you tell it's me under all this gook?" Peter asked John.

"Uh-uh," John answered. "I thought it was Frankenstein."

Peter sat down and flipped through a comic book from back to front. He whistled the "March" from the *Nutcracker* between his teeth.

"Cut it out," John said. "It's supposed to be bad luck to whistle before a performance."

"Oh," said Peter. He hummed instead. Then he jumped up, and holding onto the back of his chair, he began his warm-up *pliés*, spreading his knees wide apart as he bent them, keeping his back straight and his chest high. He had been exercising his injured ankle for several days, on Dr. Shultz's orders, and now he had to recall the feel of the crutches under his arms to remember which ankle had been hurt. The *pliés* made his muscles feel firm and packed with energy.

"John," said Peter, "can you come over after the performance? We're having a party."

"Sure," John answered without looking up from his comic book. "Just remind me to call home."

Peter was the first boy to get into his costume, and the first one out the door when the call came to go on stage. Under his makeup and costume he was ready to explode with excitement. His eyes shone, but he didn't say a word as they all climbed the stairs.

The other boys talked loudly about Christmas presents and vacation plans, and about how much snow was expected to fall. In their velvet jackets, silk bow ties, and lace cuffs they looked like proper little gentlemen, but they sounded like any other gang of kids.

"Quiet it down," said Mr. Corbin as they entered the backstage area. Muffled applause came through the closed curtain. Then the overture began.

"I'm so sick of that music I could die," said someone behind Peter. Voices groaned in agreement.

"Okay. Places," directed Mr. Corbin.

As the applause for the overture died away and the curtain rose, Peter was nearly blinded by the sudden glare of the spotlights. Looking out at the house, he could see nothing at first but the glowing red exit signs. But even though he couldn't see the audience, he could sense it out there, filling the theater like an enormous, invisible creature, breathing and coughing in the blackness. Then he noticed Mr. Green's face, shining in the yellow light from his music stand. Peter was happy just to be near him.

The music, which seemed more familiar to Peter than his own name, had already set him in motion like a wind-up toy. He was dancing at last.

At first it seemed to Peter, as he smiled and pretended to play at the Christmas party, that things were happening too fast. It was like being in an old silent movie, with everything speeded up and jerky. The vividness of the sights and sounds on stage was astonishing. Red, yellow, and blue bulbs overhead gave off a blaze of hot, white light. The electric candles on the Christmas tree flickered and flared in a syncopated rhythm. As the girls danced, their silk costumes shimmered, blending in shifting harmonies of rich color. Spotlight beams danced through the air onto the stage. The orchestra sounded fresh and bright, almost brash. Peter felt dizzy with excitement, as though he were spinning inside a giant kaleidoscope.

"Hey, take it easy!" whispered Lisa through smiling red lips. She looked beautiful, in a peach-colored dress trimmed with blue velvet that matched Peter's jacket. Peter was so happy to be holding her soft hand again that he had swung her around too hard, and she had nearly bumped into Elizabeth and Philip. Elizabeth smiled, too, but her eyes flashed a warning to Peter. He struggled to calm himself. He knew that although he couldn't see the audience, the audience could see every detail of his performance. One mistake by him could spoil it for everyone on stage.

123

As the "March" music began, Peter suddenly felt as though a hand had reached down and grabbed him by the stomach. He was sweating under his velvet jacket. What if he fell again after the *tour en l'air*? He had rubbed his shoes extra hard in the rosin box so they wouldn't be slippery. Now he began the *échappé* right smack on the beat and did the *sous-sous, changement, sous-sous* without a wobble. Landing firmly on both feet after the *royale*, he spotted straight ahead with his eyes and took off for the *tour en l'air*. He was up and around in a flash, and safely back on the ground.

Peter no longer had to pretend to enjoy himself at the ballet's Christmas party because, in reality, he was having a wonderful time. He had never felt more alive in his life. There was nowhere else in the whole world that he would have rather been than right there on that stage. He hoped George was out in the audience, watching him. He wished he could see his parents. During a pause in the dancing, he looked toward the section of the playhouse where he knew they were seated and grinned.

He threw himself into playing with his toy trumpet and chasing and pushing the girls. When he danced, he let himself be carried along by the music. It seemed to be a perfect performance. He only wished he had a bigger part. It would be more fun to be Fritz. He watched Fritz fight with Clara over the toy nutcracker. Fritz grabbed the nutcracker and threw it onto the stage in mock anger. With alarm, Peter saw its head break off and slide across the stage, almost into the orchestra pit. Fritz must have thrown it too hard. They were just supposed to pretend that the nutcracker was broken. The line between real and pretend was dangerously thin. "Ooooo," gasped children in the audience. Did they know that something had gone wrong? Who would retrieve the nutcracker's head? Suddenly, Peter was very glad that he wasn't Fritz.

Old Dr. Drosselmeyer, Fritz and Clara's godfather, hobbled across the stage and deftly scooped up the nutcracker's head, then returned to pick up its body. He moved quickly, but like a spritely old man, not a panicky dancer. He bound the two parts of the nutcracker tightly together with his handkerchief and handed them to Clara. She hugged her wounded nutcracker, then tenderly placed it in her doll's bed. She wasn't behind the music by even a single measure.

When the Christmas party was over, Peter hated to leave the stage. The best parts, the magical scenes, were yet to come.

At least I can do it again tomorrow, he consoled himself as he bowed to Fritz and Clara and their parents, and walked into the cool, dark wings. Reluctantly, he went downstairs to his dressing room, where he had plenty of time to read John's comic books while he waited to take his curtain call at the end of Act I.

"Well, was it worth it?" John asked Peter as the curtain closed for the third time and the applause finally died away.

"Was it worth it?" Peter repeated. "Boy, was it worth it! It was worth anything." Then he remembered it all—his feeling of shame that he was different from other boys because he loved ballet, the fear that his secret would be found out, the terror he felt the day of the snowball fight, the car sickness, the pain in his ankle. It had almost been too much to bear. Then he remembered the sweet triumph of knowing that one of his snowballs had turned Dalton's cheek to red mush, the pleasure of being praised by his father for his courage and by Mr. Corbin for his dancing, and the wonderful experience he had while watching Mr. Green play the celesta. It was hard to believe that so much had happened since he decided to try out for the *Nutcracker* just three months ago.

"You know something funny?" John said as they walked back to their dressing room. "I get used to the problems I have because I dance, but I *never* get used to the fun of dancing on the stage. I just never do."

"I bet that's exactly how I'll feel," Peter said. "Right now, I can hardly wait to do it again tomorrow, and the day after, and then there'll be next year and the year after . . ."

"Until you get too big and they can't use you any more," John added.

Peter laughed. "I'm going to get out of this costume and get the gook off my face, then go find George, my friend from school," he said. "Wait for me here when the show is over."

Peter stood in the back of the theater to watch the last half of Act II. When the performance was over, he spotted George standing uncertainly near the kettledrums. Peter pushed his way down the aisle against the tide of people surging up the aisle.

"Hey, George! Hi!" he yelled. He no longer cared who saw him. In fact, he hoped that everyone who saw him knew that he was the boy in the blue velvet jacket who danced in Act I. "I was hoping you'd make it," he said when he reached George. "Did you see me dance?"

"At first I couldn't tell which one was you," George said. "But then I recognized you by the way you smile. It sure looked like you were having fun. How do you remember all that stuff?"

"Oh, it's easy," said Peter with a shrug. "Come on backstage and I'll show you everything."

Peter led George through a door, up a few stairs, and into the wings. He pointed out the lighting switchboard and the expandable Christmas tree, which was already being lowered into place for the next performance.

"Hey, Pete!" called a man's voice. "We missed you backstage." Freddy emerged from behind the candy-cane throne and slapped Peter on the back. "How's the leg?" he asked.

"Great," said Peter. "This is my friend, George. George, Freddy." They shook hands. No one could think of anything else to say, so they all just stood there, smiling at each other.

"Well, we've got to go now," said Peter finally. "I'll see you tomorrow, Freddy."

"You bet, Pete," said Freddy, and he hit Peter on the back again.

"You remember the Arabian dancer I told you about?" Peter asked George. "The guy who does judo and karate?" George nodded. "That's him," Peter said, pointing to a man who was practicing turns in the center of the stage. "Want to meet him?"

The man was dark-skinned, bearded, and very tall and muscular. He wore billowing purple silk pants trimmed with sequins, and a yellow turban. He came to a sudden stop, panting and scowling, his enormous hands on his hips.

"Maybe we'd better not bother him," George whispered. "He looks ferocious."

Catching sight of Peter watching him from the edge of the stage, a big smile flashed across the dancer's face.

"Hey, man," he growled. "Don't hang back. Glad to see you're off those sticks. Who's that dude?" he asked, looking at George.

"Uriah, this is my friend George, from school." To George he said, "You know Johnson's Gym, downtown?" George nodded. "Well, this is him, Uriah Johnson."

Uriah stuck out his hand, and George shyly put out his. As they shook, George thought he felt a bone crunch.

"Come around to the gym anytime, guys. But right now, man, I've got to whip this turn into shape." Uriah planted himself firmly in fifth position and stared straight ahead. Then he extended his arm and pointed one foot to the side. Drawing his foot in quickly, he crouched for a moment in a *plié,* then took off like a human top.

"What did I tell you?" said Peter proudly as he and George walked into the wings.

"He sure doesn't look like a—"

George was interrupted by a woman's voice wailing, "My hair, my hair! It is lost!"

Natalie Roberge, still wearing her Sugar Plum Fairy costume, but with her own close-cropped hair showing, was searching backstage for her wig.

"Peter, Peter," she said. "Do you know where is my hair? I took it off." She tugged at her own hair as though she were going to pull it off. "I was so hot! But now it is gone. Gone! How was the dancing?" she asked, pausing for a moment. "Good? Good." She patted his cheek lightly.

"Here it is, sweetheart!" called one of the stagehands. He handed her a mass of black hair. She kissed the wig, then the man. With a wave to Peter she was gone.

George looked stunned. "They sure aren't the kind of people I thought they'd be," he said.

"Come on," said Peter. "I have to get my stuff in the dressing room, and my friend John is waiting."

He led George through the backstage maze and downstairs to the boys' dressing room. Everyone had left except John.

"I thought you'd forgotten you asked me," John said.

Peter introduced George to John and explained that he had been showing George around.

"Don't I know you from somewhere?" John asked. "What school do you go to? Oh, I know," he said, before George could answer. "Swimming."

George looked blank.

"Those lessons at the 'Y'," John said.

George's face suddenly lit up. "Oh, yeah," he said. "I remember. You were the kid who did the dead man's float a foot below the surface."

"Yeah," said John. "That's me all right. When I tread, only my eyes are above water."

"But you're fast," George said. "You won in the freestyle, didn't you? You look different now," he added. "I guess it's because you're dry."

Peter whistled softly as he collected his things and led his friends upstairs to the stage door. His parents, Pearson, Elizabeth, and Sharon were waiting. The man on the stool had let the grown-ups in to keep warm, but he wouldn't let them enter the inner sanctum of the backstage area.

As they trooped out into the still, icy air, Peter linked his arm through his father's, and John and George linked arms and hooked onto Peter. They kicked up clouds of soft snow and breathed out clouds of mist as they laughed. Sharon and Elizabeth joined the chain, and they played crack the whip all the way to the car.

The three grownups squeezed into the front seat, and with considerable moaning and giggling, all five children squeezed into the back.

"You want to know what I think about ballet now, sports fan?" Pearson asked Peter right away, before the car was warmed up.

"I don't know if I do or not," Peter answered, hoping Pearson wasn't going to embarrass him in front of his friends.

"Well, I'm going to tell you anyway. I think that was one heck of a terrific show. It had everything—music, costumes, lots of action. It even had all those pretty girls in short little tutus or whatever you call them. I really enjoyed it, and it looked as though you did, too."

"I sure did," Peter said. "Did you see what happened to the nutcracker's head? It was nearly a disaster."

"I thought that was supposed to happen," Pearson said.

"That's nothing," Sharon said. "Did you see what happened in the second act?" She described how one of the little clowns had gotten left behind on the stage. The children talked the rest of the way home about every detail of the performance—things that were better than ever, and mistakes that no one but dancers would notice.

By the time they had pulled off their boots, hung up their coats, and started a fire roaring in the fireplace, mugs of hot apple cider and a platter piled high with warm cinnamon doughnuts were ready.

"We need some popcorn," said Peter. "I still think ballet and popcorn go together."

They found the popcorn popper, poured in some cooking oil and a cupful of popping corn, then took turns holding it over the fire. Soon they could hear the oil sputtering, then the muffled explosions of popping corn.

"It's ready," said John.

"No, it's not," said Sharon. "It's still popping."

"It's burning," said Peter. "Hurry! Dump it out!"

The soft white puffs filled a large wooden salad bowl to the brim. Only a few burned kernels stuck to the bottom of the pop-per. Elizabeth poured on melted butter and sprinkled salt on top. Then everyone grabbed a handful and settled back in front of the fire. Peter sighed with contentment.

"So, what do you say, sports fan?" Pearson asked Peter. "Are you going to be a ballet dancer when you grow up?"

"I don't know," Peter answered. "Maybe. Or I might be some kind of a 'gist' instead."

Pearson looked puzzled.

"You know," said Peter, stuffing some more popcorn into his mouth. "Something that ends in 'gist,' like an archeologist, or a geologist, or a zoologist. I like animals and rocks and things. But maybe—if I get to be good enough—I'll be a dancer. I still have a while to think about it. Right now, it's just something I love to do, and I'm glad I don't have to sneak around to do it any more. I hate sneaking—even into football games."

"When did you sneak into a football game?" Elizabeth gasped. "Mom, Peter snuck into a football game."

"Don't blame me," Peter said. "It was Dad's idea—right, Dad?"

Peter's father got up and poked the fire with the long-handled iron shovel. A shower of sparks fell from the logs, and the fire flared up. Peter couldn't tell if his father was laughing or angry when he turned around, his face flushed, and said, "Peter, just when I'm feeling so proud of you, do you have to spoil it by telling all my secrets?"

"Sorry, Dad," Peter said. "I didn't know it was a secret."

"Well," his father said with a laugh, "it's not exactly *my* secret. I just said that when I was your age 'kids' did it. I never said *I* did it. Actually, I was too scared to try!"

Peter thought he saw his father glance at Pearson, who was talking to Elizabeth. Maybe Pearson was the kind of kid who snuck into and out of things, and maybe that was one of his little secrets. It tickled Peter's imagination to picture his father and Pearson as childhood buddies. He wondered if he and George would still be best friends when they were grown up, and if Elizabeth would still be trying to tell on him when she was a hundred and he was still only ninety-eight.

"I *know* I want to be a dancer when I grow up," Elizabeth was saying to Pearson. "But it all depends on being good enough, and you don't know if you can be good enough until you really try. With dancing, you can't wait till you're a grownup to decide. By then it's too late to train your body."

"You sound like you're training for the Olympics," Pearson said.

"I guess it *is* like that," Elizabeth said. "Right after vacation I'm starting to take Madame's extra *pointe* class. She said I was getting strong enough." She crossed her legs and pointed her toes, hoping Pearson would notice her firm leg muscles.

"You mean you'll be taking ballet three times a week?" Sharon asked. "That won't leave you time to have any fun."

"It all depends on what your idea of fun is," Elizabeth answered.

"That's not mine," Sharon said firmly. "In fact, I might as well tell you now—I'm quitting. Ballet makes my legs ache and my feet hurt, and I'm getting tired of it, anyway. But guess who's starting to take lessons."

"Who?" Elizabeth said.

"My mother, that's who," Sharon said. "Since she's the one who thinks ballet is so great, I told her she should do it and leave me alone. So she is."

"Maybe you should take it up, old man," Pearson said to Peter's father, jabbing him with his elbow and laughing.

"What's so funny about that?" Peter's father asked. "But I'm with Sharon," he added. "It looks like too much hard work to be fun. I think I'll just stick to watching. You know, these days I'm beginning to feel that way about basketball, too. Must be old age."

Pearson snorted. "I still think ballet dancing is a pretty funny thing for a man to do."

"That's the same way my father feels," said John, who had been sitting near the fire eating popcorn and listening. "Only *he* won't even come to watch—not even once. You don't know how lucky you are, Peter."

"Well, *we* watched you," Peter's father said, "and you weren't bad—for a boy!"

Peter threw a piece of popcorn at John, who caught it and laughed.

"Come on, sports fans!" Pearson said. "Who wants to go out and play a little ball? Hurry up. Get your coats on. It's getting dark."

In his jacket pocket, Peter found a rolled-up *Nutcracker* program. "Catch, Lizzie," he said, tossing it to his sister. "Put it in with last year's."

"Who are you going to be next year?" Elizabeth asked him.

"Fritz," Peter said without stopping to think. "And you're going to be Clara."

Elizabeth looked pleased. "I won't be good enough to be Clara by next year," she said. "But maybe in a few years . . ." She smiled.

Everyone went outside. As always, Pearson pretended to sink a couple of golf balls into imaginary holes. Then he slugged out several home runs with an invisible ball and bat. They all cheered. He caught the real football from Peter's father and threw it to Peter. The ball slipped between Peter's hands and landed in the snow.

"What's the matter?" Pearson yelled. "Can't you butter-fingered ballerinas even catch a ball?"

Peter laughed and threw the ball in a high, clean arc, right over Pearson's head, to his father.

"Next time, why don't you try getting off the ground with a little *jeté,* Pearson?" Peter yelled back.

They passed the ball around until the snow made it too slippery to play with. Then they all threw snowballs at each other instead.

F
Sim

Simon, Marcia L   7972

Special gift